A Ballad for Sallie

A Ballad
for Sallie

JUDY ALTER

A DOUBLE D WESTERN

DOUBLEDAY

New York   London   Toronto   Sydney   Auckland

A DOUBLE D WESTERN
PUBLISHED BY DOUBLEDAY
a division of Bantam Doubleday Dell Publishing Group, Inc.
666 Fifth Avenue, New York, New York 10103

DOUBLE D WESTERN, DOUBLEDAY,
and the portrayal of the letters DD
are trademarks of Doubleday, a division of
Bantam Doubleday Dell Publishing Group, Inc.

Library of Congress Cataloging-in-Publication Data

Alter, Judy. 1938–
    A ballad for Sallie / Judy Alter. — 1st ed.
      p.   cm. — (A Double D western)
      I. Title.
    PS3551.L765B35   1992
    813'.54—dc20   92-6870

ISBN 0-385-42076-5
Printed in the United States of America
September 1992
First Edition

10 9 8 7 6 5 4 3 2 1

For Jeanne Williams, with thanks
for being both teacher and good friend

A Ballad for Sallie

One

THIS IS ABOUT HEROES, and what happens to them when they become real people. Longhair Jim Courtright was a hero in my eyes, just as he was to most everyone in Hell's Half Acre, and he'd probably always have loomed larger than life to me if only he hadn't ridden into town on the stage with Miss Sallie McNutt, newly come from Tennessee to find her kin. And if that hadn't happened, I'd still be living in Hell's Half Acre . . . or working for Lulabelle . . . or worse. But it's a long story.

In December 1885, Stephen McNutt's murder was on every tongue in Fort Worth, from the saloons of the Acre to the fine houses on the bluff. In Texas, men were shot and killed for a lot of reasons, like a drink of whisky or a bet gone wrong or a steer that strayed—none of them, I always thought, worth killing a person. But Mr. McNutt was a good man, a merchant who'd sold canned tomatoes and saddles and grain and sardines to all those cowboys who went up the trail. He was found, stabbed to death, in his store, his ledger of accounts in front of him and the cash register emptied. Judd Ambrose, just hired to clean and sweep the store, hadn't been seen since. A clear case, the tongues said, of robbery and cold-blooded murder. A noose was waiting for Ambrose whenever he was found.

But that was in December and by early February, Ambrose was still missing and the tongues of Fort Worth were occupied with other things. Stephen McNutt was pretty much forgotten— until Longhair Jim Courtright happened to arrive with Sallie Mc-

Nutt. No, they didn't actually come together, but they were on the same stage . . . and clearly, Longhair Jim wished they were together.

Ben Boy, July, and I were the first ones to see her, but only because old Red Moriarity, who drove the coach from the Texas & Pacific station to town, skipped his stop on the square and came straight to Lulabelle Browning's house in the Acre. I still think he did that on purpose because Longhair Jim was on that coach, in disguise of course, but nobody was supposed to know that. Still, we knew. Nothing Marshal Timothy Isaiah Courtright did surprised anyone, not even when he had a New Mexico murder warrant on his head. Longhair Jim could get away with things that would have had ordinary men in the hoosegow—or dead.

Red didn't often have passengers like Sallie, and I guess that's why he hollered down for someone to "help that there lady out now." Longhair Jim did as he was told, jumping out of the coach and holding both his hands up trying to grab her around the waist and help her down. But Sallie brushed his arms down, with a gesture so gentle and quick no one but Jim—and me—realized he'd been turned away. Then ever so sweetly she took his one hand, as though he'd offered it, and got down out of that smelly old coach. Longhair Jim looked thoroughly confused.

She was a big lady, almost as tall as Longhair Jim, and while she wasn't fat by any stroke, she was what some folks call sturdy. Yet somehow she managed still to look like a lady. Her hair was piled on her head but neatly, not in the mass of un-combed curls that Lulabelle favored, and she wore a plain gray traveling dress, with a fully gathered skirt and a tight-fitting bod-ice with a great splash of lace at her throat. Lulabelle would have flounced fourteen petticoats getting out of that coach, but Sallie showed no ankle or ruffle. She just got out like a lady, smiling ever so slightly.

But the smile on her face faded most as soon as she hit the ground. For one thing, a pack of hogs had taken that moment to wallow in some mud directly across the road from the coach.

They rooted and snorted in pure contentment. Even if they hadn't been there, the Acre always smelled like a place where hogs would root, and this day was no exception. It was cold, but the sun shone brightly enough to raise the smell of sewage from the open trench running down the side of the street.

I think the thing that most got Sallie was that Maudie Wingo, one of the girls who lived with Lulabelle, chose that moment to walk out the door of the house, clutching a Japanese-print kimono about her. Her hair was just barely combed and the make-up on her face was so bright you knew she wasn't a proper lady. Sallie looked at the pigs and then at Maudie and finally back at the stage as though she would get in again, but the way was blocked by a fat drummer who was getting out and wouldn't budge for anything.

"Who's that?" Ben Boy whispered, pulling on my skirt to demand an answer and pointing to make sure I knew who he meant.

"Shut up, Ben Boy," I said, knocking the offending finger away. "Don't you know it's bad manners to point?"

"Nobody ever told me," he muttered.

Longhair Jim offered Sallie his arm with a flourish, and we could hear him say, "Ma'am, you seem to have ended up in the wrong part of town. May I escort you to your destination?" He stood just barely taller than her, a thin man with that famous yellow hair curling about his shoulders and a mustache to match, and his trademark holster with two guns worn butt forward. He was still handsome, though he must have been near forty years old and had begun to slump a little. Now, his black suit was rumpled from the ride, and if I'd looked clearly, I'd have seen there was a worried look creeping in behind the brave front he was putting on for Sallie McNutt. But all I saw was the great gunfighter helping a pretty lady in distress. It was the stuff of dreams to an Acre brat.

Jim Courtright had been marshal of Fort Worth for three years or so back when I was but a little button, in the late '70s, so Lulabelle told me. He was known as a fast draw, and even shootists feared him. He'd kept the law in Fort Worth—murderers, train robbers, and horse thieves got their just deserts from Longhair Jim. But not gamblers. He had a fondness for gambling. And when the New Mexico law had come calling for Longhair Jim about an old murder charge, he'd spent two years as a fugitive. Now he was back, but he was no longer marshal, and he was probably no longer so sure of his power in Fort Worth. But those of us who lived on the streets in the Acre thought him a hero.

Sallie looked uncertain for just a minute, and then she spotted us. We must have made a sight: one twelve-year-old boy, filthy dirty, still clutching his bootblack box; a seven-year-old black girl who refused to let go of my hand, no matter how hard I tugged; and me, Lizzie Jones, fourteen years old and by my own judgment pretty plain in appearance, not to mention the ragged dress Lulabelle insisted was good for at least another year. I wasn't ashamed of who I was or where I lived, make no mistake about that. But I was a mite bothered by the way my dress fit too tight across the chest and hung too short at the ankles.

"Could you help me, please?" Longhair Jim might as well never have spoken. Sallie was looking directly at me. "I seem to be lost."

"Yes, ma'am," I said, stepping forward. If I had been taught few manners in my life, I'd had obedience drummed into me. It always avoided trouble to act like you were going to obey adults. And now I stood in front of her, silent, waiting for her to tell me what she wanted. And somewhere way in the back of my head, a small voice told me I wanted to learn to be like this lady. 'Course the logical front part of my mind knew that was impossible.

"Is that a boarding house?" She nodded her head toward Lulabelle's, and I turned to look at the familiar building. I tried to see it with Sallie's eyes, and I thought maybe it could have been a respectable boarding house. It was a large, two-story clapboard with a long verandah and the paint was fairly new—not perfect but not yet peeling. The windows had bead drapes just like you saw in big houses in the better part of town. But there was that lamp in the window, large and red, and there was Maudie, still wandering about the verandah.

Lulabelle's house had been home to me for several years, ever since Ma had gotten tired to death of life on a hardscrabble farm down south. She'd left Pa a note one day, and taken me to Fort Worth with her, where we ended up at Lulabelle's. I was loved and petted by all the girls during the day and ignored at night. When I was little, I could remember being put on a pallet in the kitchen to sleep while noisy parties went on in the parlor.

But then a couple of years ago, Ma had tired of Lulabelle's and taken off with a fancy city man, a gambler they said. She told me she'd send for me, but Lulabelle said not to count on it. I wasn't particularly upset or hurt by Ma's leaving, 'cause life had already taught me to accept what came my way. And being left behind just seemed another jog in an already crooked road.

Besides, I wasn't alone long. Just about then, I found Ben Boy living in a shack behind Lulabelle's, and I decided that was a better place to live. Lulabelle still watched over me, with about half an eye.

But now this lady, a real lady, wanted to know if Lulabelle's was a boarding house. "Not exactly," I said. "A lot of girls live there, and . . . Lulabelle Browning, she owns it. . . ."

"Lady, you don't want to stay in the Acre." Ben Boy spoke with the bluntness that I feared.

"The Acre?" It was a natural question.

"Hell's Half Acre," Ben Boy said condescendingly. "It's where we all live, but you . . ."

Sallie looked around again, and my eyes followed the turn of her head. What she saw must have been puzzling. There was Uncle Billy Winder's Cattle Exchange. A big sign with a steer on it fooled no one into thinking it was a building that had much to do with cattle, with its swinging doors and velvet curtains that could be seen through dirty windows. And even in midday, we could hear loud laughter and the sound of a tinny piano coming from inside.

Across the street and down was the Tivoli Dance Hall, a great big square wooden building without window or decoration, except for the sign that clearly said what it was. Beyond that you could see a line of one-room shacks, most in such poor repair that a strong breeze would blow them over. Usually their state didn't matter—nobody lived in one of them for long, for one reason or another. No, it wasn't the hogs and the open sewer trench that set the Acre apart. Those were found all over town. It was the people of the Acre—and the things they did for pleasure and for profit.

All of us, staring at Sallie, had forgotten about Red Moriarity and the coach. Nobody paid any attention as he threw down Jim's baggage, and sure no one noticed that he followed it with Sallie's. All we knew was that suddenly we heard a holler at the horses and a crack of the reins, and he was off down the street. The fat drummer, having also looked at the surroundings of the Acre, had quickly climbed back inside.

Sallie stared after the coach, amazed that it would leave her. But her look was not one of dismay, as you might expect from a lady abandoned in a place like the Acre. No, she was angry, and I admired her for that. Red had better hope he didn't run into her soon.

"I'm looking for Stephen McNutt," she said directly, turning toward me. "Can you point me to his store?"

"McNutt's store!" Ben Boy exploded in amazement, and even silent July grabbed my skirt tighter.

Longhair Jim had been watching us none too pleased—if we admired him, it wasn't a mutual thing. Now he stepped in. "Ah, was . . . is Mr. McNutt an acquaintance of yours, ma'am?"

"As a matter of fact, he's my cousin . . . well, the cousin of my late husband. I've come to work in his store. He was kind enough to send for me . . . but never mind, you don't need my life history. If you'll just direct me to the store, please."

Jim was gallant. He almost bowed as he said, "I'm sure your life story would be fascinating, ma'am, but I'm afraid I have bad news for you. I've only arrived in town myself, as you well know, but word had reached me ahead of a tragic incident in this city. . . ."

"Why is he talking so funny?" Ben Boy whispered, but I kicked him into silence. Sometimes I really admired Ben Boy for his ability to take care of himself, but other times I felt like he needed a keeper. This was one of those latter times.

Sallie stared intently at Longhair Jim, so he continued. "Mr. McNutt has been murdered."

"Murdered!" She was appropriately shocked, but she gave no sign of tears or hysterics, much to my relief.

"Judd Ambrose did it," Ben Boy said, reveling in the chance to tell all he knew to someone who'd listen, "and now he's disappeared but Lulabelle says he's not smart enough to murder anyone anyway. The marshal says, though, he'll find him and hang him, 'cause Mr. McNutt was an important man. Rich, real rich."

Longhair Jim and I both turned to stare at Ben Boy, who took the hint that he'd spoken out of turn and edged himself behind me, as though to hide with July in my skirts.

"Mr. Ambrose was in Mr. McNutt's employ, as I understand it," Jim said, "but his guilt is much in doubt, to my mind." He cleared his throat to emphasize the weight of his opinion. "I know this must be a grievous shock to you, ma'am, to hear the news of the loss of a loved one in such bold manner."

"I'd never met Stephen McNutt," she said without hesitation. "He only wrote me with this job offer after my husband's death."

"He was a good man," Longhair Jim said solemnly, though I doubted he'd ever met Stephen McNutt, and I wasn't sure he'd recognize a good man anyway. Just because he was a hero didn't make me blind to some things about Longhair Jim, including the fact that he was well known—and generally liked—on the shady side of the law.

Sallie did not seem to know what to do next. She stood with her chin in her hand for a long moment, and we all watched, paralyzed, while she thought. Then, briskly, she said to me, "Well, I have to find a place to stay and this"—she nodded her head toward Lulabelle's—"does not seem appropriate. Will you direct me?"

I think Longhair Jim was about to step forward and take over the directing, no matter what Sallie wanted, but Maudie Wingo chose that moment to scream, "Longhair Jim! It's you!" With that, she clutched the kimono tighter about her and came off the verandah, heading straight for our group. You don't often see panic on the face of a gunfighter, but that's the only word for the look on Jim's face. He might have come to the Acre to see Maudie, but finding more interesting things—Sallie—he most definitely didn't want Maudie Wingo screaming out his name in the street.

"Take her to Peer's House," he commanded me, and I nodded though I thought he must have spoken before he thought. Peer's House was the fanciest hotel in all of Fort Worth. I knew without asking that it was too much money for a lady whose prospects had just been wiped out by murder. I'd take her to Mrs. Straight's boarding house, though it bothered me some to disobey Longhair Jim. I was, as I said, used to obeying.

"Ben, you take July to the shack," I said, prying the little girl's hand loose from my skirts and tucking it determinedly into Ben's hand. She looked up at me, lower lip trembling, and I could see the wail building in her throat. "July," I said sternly, "if you cry, I'll wallop you *hard.*"

As they straggled away, Ben Boy dragging July, who still stared over her shoulder at us, Sallie stepped forward and held out her hand. "I'm Sallie McNutt," she said.

"Pleased to meetcha," I mumbled, awkward about holding out my hand. "I'm Lizzie Jones." Nobody had taught me manners, and I was acutely aware of my lack in that department.

Without another word, she reached to pick up her bags. She had three, and she tried to pick up all of them.

"I can take two of those," I said. "It's a long walk. . . . We could take the trolley partway."

"I've had enough of smelly coaches and the like," she said strongly, picking up two bags and starting off down the street fast enough that I had to grab the third bag in a hurry and scoot to catch up with her.

We headed down Rusk Street, dodging mudholes and ruts as we went. In 1885, Fort Worth was a growing city, stretching from the bluff clear back a mile or more to the T&P railroad tracks. Our path across town would take us down Main Street, almost to the stone courthouse, then west along Third Street for a bit, and finally north again to the bluff. Nellie Straight's boarding house sat right on the bluff, where she could look out over the prairie and watch the cattle when the great herds headed north. Nellie always said it comforted her to see the cattle go through town.

If I had been a stranger, I'd probably have thought Fort Worth was dirty and loud—men hollered at each other trying to sell everything from a wagonload of buffalo hides to sorghum made at the mill to the east of town, carriages rattled, horses neighed, dogs barked, the trolley lumbered by, music poured out of saloons, and when there was a fire huge bells rang all over town. Even as we walked, men on horseback rode by, the horses' hooves kicking up piles of dust in our direction, and men in boots and rough clothes brushed by us on the wooden sidewalk. Businessmen in fine suits also passed us, a few tipping their hats to Sallie as they went by. She smiled, ever so slightly, but kept her eyes straight ahead.

We left the Acre behind us, passing scattered residences like the brick house Mr. Boaz had built ten years ago or more, giving the town its first two-story house, and the newer and grander residence of Dr. Feild, with its verandahs on each floor and gingerbread trim along the roof line. Sallie walked briskly but my long legs made it fairly easy for me to keep up with her. And as she walked, she sang softly to herself, a song I'd never heard about a girl named Barb'ra Allen. Singing was not something anyone I knew ever did. Oh, I heard the loud noise coming from Lulabelle's parlor at night or out the door of the Tivoli, but not music like this, kind of all at once sad and happy. As we walked, I looked at her every once in a while to see if she was

self-conscious about singing, but it was like she didn't even realize she was doing it. I admired that.

In no time, we reached the business district and began to pass
stores—Sanger's Cheap Cash Store, Kuhn the bootmaker's shop,
Want and Hartsfields' where they made the fanciest cakes you
can imagine. Ben and I had drooled over the ones in the window more than once, though it didn't seem likely we'd ever do
more than deliver one to Lulabelle, who'd hide us if we sneaked
a crumb. There was Mitchell and Thurman, where they repaired
furniture, and Henry Miller who sold Howe sewing machines.
Sallie's step slowed there, and she stared long and hard at the
machine in the window until Mr. Miller himself came out the
door.

"Fine machine, that," he said. "Care to try it today, little lady?"

"No, no thanks, not today." And she was off down the street
again. I wondered if she knew by instinct where we were going,
for she never asked me for directions, and she was generally in
the lead. She did ask one question.

"Where is Mr. McNutt's store?"

"A block over," I said, "on Throckmorton."

"Can we see it?" I shrugged. Where we went was up to her, so
we turned on Fifth and went a block out of our way to see
Stephen McNutt's store. He had called it McNutt's Mercantile and
Supplies, and the windows on either side of the double doors
displayed all the things he sold—saddles and bridles, coffee by
the sack, shirts to wear, and canned goods to eat. A big sign on
the door said CLOSED.

Sallie stepped up to the door and cupped her hands around
her eyes to look inside. "It's awfully dark and gloomy," she said.
"Probably dirty by now too." Then she noticed a smaller sign in
one window. "Walter Lambreth, attorney-at-law," she read. "Do
you know him?"

"No, ma'am," I replied. In the Acre, one didn't exactly run into
fancy lawyers all the time, and if you did, you knew not to ever
mention it.

"I guess I will have to send word to Mr. Lambreth that I've arrived in town."

"Yes, ma'am," I said, "but we best get to Mrs. Straight's before suppertime."

"Mrs. Straight's? I thought we were going to Peer's House."

"We can, but that's a hotel, ma'am, a fancy hotel, with female waiters in the dining room and great white tablecloths on each table. It's grand."

"I can't afford a grand hotel."

"You wouldn't like it nohow. The lobby is always full of fat drummers who sell patent medicine and sit around telling tall tales about their adventures in the wild land of Texas."

She laughed then, a deep laugh, and I knew she was special.

"Mrs. Straight's got a boarding house over on Belknap. You'll like it fine. We'll turn on the next street."

We were almost to the corner when it happened. A hide freighter, his clothes baggy and stained and smelling as bad as the hides he hauled, blocked the street, hands on his hips, watching Sallie approach him.

"Pardon me," she said, trying to go around him.

He stuck out his arms to block the way, and then he looked at me. "One of the brats from the Acre, ain't ya? Get on back where ya belong. I'll see to the lady." He reached for Sallie, as though to put an arm around her, but she was too quick for him. Her dodge left him off balance and he came close to tumbling to the ground.

"Takin' on airs, huh?" he grunted, righting himself. "I'll show ye who's too good for who!" And he lunged in her direction again.

I stuck my foot directly out in his path. This time, he hit the dirt hard, sprawling face down on the rough street and coughing as the rising dust filled his mouth. One thing I'd learned well in the Acre was not to let the other person win the bluff. Fear often got you a black eye or a beating, but boldness rarely did. I walked around the fallen man to stand directly in front of his face.

"This lady's a real lady," I said. "You leave her alone or I'll call Marshal Courtright."

"He ain't even here," the freighter muttered, shaking his head to clear it.

"Ha! Fat lot you know about it. Just go on down to Lulabelle Browning's if you don't think he's here. Now get on out of our way."

He rose, brushed at his clothes as though they weren't dusty and dirty enough before he fell, and walked away, muttering something about all women looking alike.

Sallie had been silent and still during this exchange. I expected she'd be about to faint from fear, but she wasn't. She simply watched the man stumble away and then turned to me. "How'd you know he wouldn't take out after you?"

"I just knew," I said. How did you explain the instinct for survival that the Acre bred? "He's not . . . well, he doesn't live here. I wouldn't want you to think Fort Worth is all like him."

"Heavens, we had men like that in Tennessee, especially after the War." She laughed. "They may have worn different clothes, and they didn't smell quite that bad, but the same type is all over."

After the War? Of course I knew about the War. It had ended a long time before I was born, maybe five years, and I thought of it as ancient history. If she could remember back to then, I thought, she must be pretty old. I wasn't much judge, but I guessed maybe Sallie was thirty-five. Anyway, I knew she wasn't exactly close to my age.

"Tennessee?" I asked.

"The green green hills of Tennessee," she said. "Near Gatlinburg."

I shook my head. It meant nothing to me except some place far away back east.

"Lived there all my life," Sallie went on. "Never thought I'd leave. But things happen, things change. I . . . well, anyway, here I am, ready for a new life, only something's happened again. Stephen McNutt's been murdered." She said it wryly, al-

most as though the murder were a good joke on her. She started
to walk, picking up the thread of the song she'd been humming.
After we turned along Belknap Street, we passed the wagon-
yard, with its dismal line of hearses—black for adults and white
for little children—and the brick kiln where it seemed the heat
would surely reach out on the street and grab us.

Sallie never did seem to tire, but I was near exhausted by the
time we reached Mrs. Straight's, and I could feel a lock of hair
sliding down my forehead. When I brushed it back, I probably
left a dirt streak. Sallie, by contrast, seemed fresh and clean and
pretty, in spite of having been on the train and in that smelly old
coach.

Mrs. Straight lived in a cottage, white frame with gingerbread
trim around the front porch and lace curtains in the window.
There was a fence around the front yard, with the usual water
barrel just inside the gate, and a wild rose bush climbed up one
of the fence posts. The roses were important—they told you that
you weren't in the Acre, you were with folks who cared about
permanence. In summer I always stopped to smell the blos-
soms, and summer or winter, I used to wish I lived in a house
just like this. Sometimes I'd let myself dream about windows
with glass in them and a kitchen with a real stove, but most
times I reckoned such dreaming didn't get you anywhere but
unhappy. Still it always cheered me to go to Nellie Straight's
house.

"Will she mind my just appearing on her doorstep?" Sallie
asked.

"No. She don't take very many boarders," I explained. "But
she'll have room for you." I jerked the bell, which hung on a
rope in front of the door, and in a minute Nellie Straight opened
the door.

"Land's sake, Lizzie, I don't need any help today." She was a
little woman, a sparrow, I always thought, because of the way
she flitted about her house, doing a hundred different things at a
time. Sometimes I cleaned house with her to earn a few extra
pennies, and her energy flat made me tired.

"I didn't come to clean, Mrs. Straight. I brought you a boarder."

"Good gracious, I don't need any more of them either!"

Rebuffed, Sallie started to turn away. But Mrs. Straight's voice stopped her. "Don't be going off in a huff. I'll make room for you, since Lizzie's brought you. Come, let me have a look at you."

Turning, Sallie stood as though for inspection. Her eyes met Mrs. Straight's burning blue stare directly.

"Just arrived in town, didn't you?"

"Yes, ma'am, I did."

"I can tell. From back east . . . maybe Tennessee."

Sallie relaxed a little and grinned. "Tennessee. How'd you know?"

"There's some that looks like Georgia, and others like Alabama, and some looks like Tennessee. You do. Come on in this house. Lizzie, you coming too?"

"No, ma'am, I got to get back. I left July with Ben."

"I got fresh bread, just out of the oven. And it's a long walk back to the Acre."

It didn't take much to convince me. We carried Sallie's bags to a tiny room near the back of the house. It was sparkling clean, and so pretty I near wanted to cry for wanting something better than the shack I shared with Ben Boy and July. The brass bed had a patchwork quilt on it, with all sorts of colors and patterns, and there were lace curtains in these windows, too, and a rag rug on the floor, its crazy colors echoing the quilt.

"You can open the windows and get that prairie breeze," Nellie told her.

We left Sallie to freshen up, as Mrs. Straight said, and went into the kitchen, where she sliced me thick pieces of warm bread, light and fluffy and not at all like the heavy old cornbread that I ate so much of. I wished Nellie were my mother, and then felt a pang of guilt about Lulabelle, who tried to be good to me. Usually I never admitted, even to myself, how much I longed for someone who did care. It was easier just to learn not to care yourself.

When Sallie came in, Nellie gave her a piece of bread and a glass of milk. Then we sat in the parlor and watched the sky to the west turn pink and red.

"Almost as pretty as Tennessee," Sally said, smiling a little.

Mrs. Straight bristled right away. "Ain't nothin' prettier than a Texas sunset over the prairie," she said. "We got a little piece of heaven here."

"Looks to me like Lizzie lives in a little piece of the other place," Sallie said quietly, while I hid my head.

"Lizzie's a good girl," Mrs. Straight said, dodging the issue. "She's goin' to be just fine." But that bony old hand reached over and rubbed my back for just a minute, as though to let me know that I, too, was special.

I nearly purred like a kitten.

It was almost dark when I left for my long walk home, but I didn't mind at all. 'Specially not when Sallie gave me a quarter and her thanks and said, "Can you come back tomorrow? I'll need a guide to find my way around town. Should I ask your mother?"

I almost laughed at her, but I managed to be polite enough. "Ma don't care," I said. "I'll come." No need to tell her I hadn't seen Ma in most two years.

On the way back to the Acre, I kept hearing that song in my mind, the one about Barb'ra Allen.

Two

JULY WAS WAITING outside the shack when I got back to the Acre. "I'm hungry," she whined, burying her head in her arm and wiping a dirty hand across her nose.

"Where's Ben Boy?" I demanded, angry that he'd left her alone.

"Gone," was all she wailed, and I gave up. July was going to have to toughen up if she expected to survive in the Acre, especially her being black. Nobody much in Fort Worth cared about us in the Acre, and they still hadn't gotten used to the first black mail carrier, though he'd been carrying mail near two years now, so July's situation—a black brat in the Acre—was double jeopardy.

"Come on, let's go find some supper. I've got a quarter." I fingered the quarter Sallie had given me, wishing it would go for ribbons instead of cheese and bread. I could sell ribbons for a pretty profit on a street corner downtown, but food was more important, even if it was sort of a onetime use of money. Maybe Ben Boy would bring a chicken, I thought.

Dinner that night was bread, cheese, and some winter squash that nobody at Lulabelle's would eat. We didn't do much better about it, though I tried to tell Ben Boy he had to eat vegetables every so often.

"Who said that?" he demanded, his mouth stuffed full of bread.

I didn't know who said it, but it sounded right to me. Ben Boy sat up cleaning his shoe rags, but I was tired, and July and I curled up on our pallet early. July, her energy exhausted from making herself invisible all day, curled herself in a ball, edged up against me, and slept soundly, but I lay awake for a long time, remembering the day, hearing in my mind the strains of "Barb'ra Allen." I fell asleep dreaming of living at Mrs. Straight's, but somewhere in the dream a tall, sinister man in a rumpled suit kept lurking in the shadows.

"You there, brat!" The loud, angry voice stopped me in the street in front of the Tivoli. July and I were on our way to Want and Hartsfields to buy a fine cake for Lulabelle. She had an enormous sweet tooth, and I earned a quarter for fetching goodies to soothe her craving.

Longhair Jim came toward me, his long legs taking huge steps and his face twisted into a scowl. "She's not at Peer's House," he said. "Where'd you take her?"

I'd long ago learned not to play dumb, though I was sorely tempted to ask, "Take who?" Still, I knew who he meant and figured a direct answer was my best choice. "To Mrs. Straight's, over on Belknap. It's cheaper than Peer's House . . . and more pleasant."

"I told you to take her to the hotel." He stood, blocking our way, and July retreated to her usual place behind me, clutching my skirt and hiding in its folds. I reached one hand around to pull her away and kept the other ready just in case I needed to ward off a quick blow.

"She didn't want to go to the hotel."

"But . . . but I have connections there. . . ." There was almost a whine in his voice, the way July sounded when she was scared. It startled me to hear that tone. Longhair Jim was supposed to be firm and bold and never ever be afraid of anything.

I looked at the ground. "You can find her at Mrs. Straight's."

"I haven't got time to go clear over there," he said importantly. "Got business to do. You go tell Miss McNutt that I'd much admire to meet with her at noon today at Peer's House."

He lowered his voice, though there was no one near to hear a word he said. "I got to tell her something important about her cousin's murder."

I stood, waiting, until he said, "Oh, all right," and dug into his pocket for a quarter.

"I can't guarantee that she'll be there," I said, and he nodded.

July stuck out her tongue at his back as he walked away, but I smacked her lightly and told her she should respect adults.

"I don't like him," she wailed.

"He's Longhair Jim Courtright," I told her sharply, as though that explained everything. But that whine in his voice lingered in my mind.

Even Lulabelle was talking about Sallie that day. When I delivered the cake—a huge one decorated with great swirls of icing and marzipan oranges—she asked me about her.

"Hear you showed a lady over to Mrs. Straight's, dearie?" Lulabelle sat up in her canopied bed, yards of gauze whirling around her from the bedposts in some kind of decoration that I always thought was a fire hazard. She had a gauzy gown, too, and the whole effect was to make her look unreal. Except Lulabelle herself was solid and real, a big woman whose layers of fat made it difficult for her to get in and out of chairs or to climb stairs. Evenings when there were parties in the front room, she just sat in one great overstuffed chair and never did get up all evening.

"Yes, ma'am," I replied. I was always polite to Lulabelle because I thought she was breakable inside that huge body. And in my own way, I was fond of her, just as she cared about me, though she sometimes had a funny way of showing it.

"Did you tell her I sometimes take in ladies looking for work?"

"No, ma'am. She's not like the ladies that live with you . . . she's, well, she's a fine lady. Had some schooling, I bet."

Lulabelle's face clouded, as though I'd hurt her feelings. "Too good for the Acre, huh?" she sniffed. "Well, I don't know what else much a woman can do in this town, alone, and I already heard all about her cousin being the one that was murdered."

News traveled fast in the Acre, and I had no doubt that Maudie had heard from Jim about Sallie being related to the late Stephen McNutt and had relayed that piece of gossip straight to Lulabelle.

"Drat," Lulabelle said suddenly, while I still stood awkwardly at the foot of the bed. "I've ripped my gown. Can't get a good seamstress these days. I suppose I'll just have to pitch it to one of the girls." Lulabelle's gown would have been a tent on any of her girls, but I kept my peace. Then she focused her attention on me.

"How old you be now, Lizzie?"

"Fourteen, ma'am."

"Ain't it about time you started earning a living?"

I knew what Lulabelle was saying, but I avoided her. "I earn enough to get by, like running errands for you. And sometimes I get some ribbons to sell. Excuse me, Miz Lulabelle, but I've got another errand to run. Mr. Courtright already paid me a quarter."

I knew Lulabelle wanted me to go to work for her—and I knew what the girls did—but I was determined not to end up like Ma. Sometimes it scared me because I couldn't see any other end ahead for me, like most girls in the Acre, but I was determined to hold on.

"Mr. Courtright!" Lulabelle sniffed again. "There's trouble come to town with that one," she predicted darkly.

"Don't know why," I said. "He's an important man."

Lulabelle just shook her head, as I ran out to the kitchen, where I'd left July munching on a homemade biscuit. Sophronia, who cooked for Lulabelle and her girls, made wonderful biscuits.

"Thanks," I said, grabbing a biscuit and heading for the door before she could yell at me. Dragging July slowed me down long enough to hear Sophronia's mutterings. "That baby seen enough trouble already," Sophronia said darkly, "what with her ma dying so suddenly. I don't see no good in her future. Ain't no decent place for a black girl in this city." Her own black skin glistened as she spoke.

"Nonsense, 'Phronie. I look after her, and she's going to be fine." July grabbed my skirt tightly, and I wished Sophronia would keep her all-seeing eye to herself, at least in front of July, who probably believed everything she said. "There, July, 'Phronie's just teasing you. You're gonna' be fine."

Still I remembered July's mother with a shudder. She'd lived with Lulabelle until it was obvious she had a bad case of consumption. Lulabelle was one of the few ladies in the Acre who didn't draw the color line, and she hadn't minded Janey's black skin, but she didn't tolerate sickness, at least not the catching kind. Thin as a rail, Janey moved to one of the tiny shacks in the Acre, taking with her this baby girl of about four. "Named her July myself," she told me once, " 'cause July's the best month. It's when I knew her pa." I never asked what happened to him.

She was too weak to care for July, let alone herself, and somehow it all fell to me and May, who lived with Lulabelle then but who since went off and married a cowboy. May tended to the mother, and I took care of July, and we were both there one day when the dying woman lay in her bed, moaning and tossing. Suddenly, though, she sat straight up and began singing "Swing Low, Sweet Chariot" in a clear, strong voice. After a verse and a half, she fell back on the bed and died.

May's responsibility extended only so far. "Guess you better take care of that baby," she said after they took Janey's body away to bury in a pauper's grave. We never could find any papers or anything to tell who to notify, and I wondered a lot about some folks somewhere who would never know what happened to her, never know their grandchild. But July had followed me around like a puppy dog ever since, and disgusted as I sometimes got, I wouldn't have abandoned her, even to save myself from the devil.

Now I took her in search of Ben Boy, so I didn't have to drag her all the way to Mrs. Straight's. I found him in the shack, getting ready to go out to the streets downtown for the day.

"Oh, Lizzie, do I got to? I'm goin' to the Metropolitan today.

Hear some cattlemen came into town yesterday, and I bet their boots is dusty to beat all."

"Ben Boy, you take her with you. She won't be trouble, and I'll fix you a cobbler tonight if you'll do it."

He eyed me suspiciously. "Cobbler?"

I nodded yes.

"All right. But if she's trouble, it's the last time." He glared at July, who stared back blankly at him.

I pried her hand loose from my skirt, gave her a hug, and said cheerfully, "Ben Boy will take you, and I'll come by the Metropolitan on the way home and get you." As I left, over my shoulder, I said to Ben Boy, "Don't forget to take some apples off a cart if you want cobbler."

I ran before he could throw a brush at me.

"Meet him at that fancy hotel?" Sallie's eyes widened when I told her of Courtright's request . . . or order, which it more was. "I don't go meeting men at hotels," she said emphatically, "but tell me who he is. Why would he think I should meet him?"

I told her about the whispered promise that he knew something about Stephen McNutt's murder, and she scoffed. "Who is he, that he would know more than the sheriff or marshal or whoever's in charge?"

So I told her all I knew, which was pretty much what everyone knew, that his name was Timothy Isaiah Courtright but everyone called him Longhair Jim, a name he'd gotten when he was in gunfighter shows and the like with his wife, and how he'd been an army scout before he was a shootist and then, after the Wild West shows, he was marshal in Fort Worth, cottoning to gamblers and being pretty fair with the cowboys who wanted to raise holy ned in the Acre before they went up the trail to Kansas. Fort Worth was the last city a South Texas cowboy saw before those long, dry months on the trail, and it was the first place he came to with money jinglin' in his pocket on the way home. Cowboys were important to the city because they brought money, and Longhair Jim treated them royally. If a

drunken cowboy shot up the streets, Jim tried to send him home
with a buddy. At the worst, he locked them up for a night, and
then let them go without a heavy fine. Courtright worked for the
city, and he knew what was good for the city treasury. But he
was also tough on highwaymen, and no one could outdraw
him.

"Most lately, he's been to South America, on account of the
New Mexico law wanted him," I said, all ready to launch into
what I thought was an exciting story.

Sallie interrupted me. "The law? Why was the law after a marshal?"

We were at the big dining table in Nellie's house, and Sallie
was mending a napkin for Nellie, her fingers taking fast but tiny
stitches even while she listened to me. And ever so faintly I
could hear her humming a refrain over and over behind the tone
of my own voice. It was a different song from the one she'd
sung yesterday.

" 'Cause he was wanted for murder," I said matter-of-factly.
And then I told her how he'd left and gone to New Mexico,
mostly because the city council wanted him to get tough with
the cowboys. They all wanted the money and business the trail
herds brought to Fort Worth, but they wanted law and order too,
and they didn't seem to understand they couldn't have both at
once.

But then he'd come back to Fort Worth to hide, accused of
murder in the silver mines of New Mexico. Seems he and a man
named Jim McIntyre had been too close when two men were
found murdered—some said Mexicans, others said Frenchmen,
and I figured it didn't matter, 'cause men were men. After that,
he was in Fort Worth for a good while, even opened his detective agency, and nobody seemed to pay any mind to the murder
warrants against him. But then one day two Texas Rangers and a
New Mexico chief of police came after him.

"It was real exciting the day they came for him," I said, getting
carried away with my story. "The rangers, they tricked Jim into
going to their hotel room, told him they needed him to identify

some pictures, and then they held him prisoner, and everyone in town turned out to protect him."

"Protect him? He'd murdered two men! Why would the town want to protect him?"

"Because he's Longhair Jim," I said, as though that explained it all, because to my mind it did. "Everybody gathered in front of the Ginnochio Hotel where they held him, and all the men had guns. They hollered that those law officers had better let Courtright go or they'd all be killed. It was exciting. I was right there, watching from the top of a shed."

Sallie looked at me a moment, and then seemed to shudder. "Did your mother let you go near a mob like that?"

"Ma didn't know," I said, figuring that wasn't really a lie. Sallie didn't understand how or where I lived. She thought I had a mother who watched after me, and probably a comfortable home to boot, and I wasn't ready to tell her different. But it had never occurred to me before that mothers kept track of where their daughters went or had any say about where you could or couldn't go. I saw Sallie shake her head.

"Anyway, they were going to take him on the night train, but first they took him to this restaurant for supper, and he dropped his napkin on the floor and bent down to pick it up, and when he straightened back up he had two six-shooters in his hands." I thought it was probably the best story I'd ever tell in my life, and I waited for her to be impressed.

Sallie stopped sewing to stare at me. "Where did he get them?"

That seemed obvious to me. "Someone hid them there for him," I explained as patiently as I could. "Folks said they served him boiled fish, quail on toast, and pistols under the table for dessert."

Sallie was not amused. "They hid pistols to help him?"

I couldn't understand why she found this so difficult. "Sure. And then they helped him get away. Folks in the restaurant covered the Rangers and the deputy or whoever he was from

New Mexico while Jim ran out and got on the horse they had
waiting for him."

"They who?"

"I don't know. Just the men that wanted to help him get
away."

She had a way of asking about the unimportant things and not
letting me get to the exciting parts. "But the horse stumbled and
nearly fell on Jim, right in front of the fire station, and he only
got away because he used to be a volunteer fireman and the
firemen were all his friends. They helped him."

"And he went away for two years and now he's back?" She
made his recent life history into a question.

"Yeah, but he was on trial in New Mexico—he finally went
back there—and they found him innocent."

"So now he's home a hero?"

"I don't know that he's a hero to everybody," I said. "He's
Longhair Jim Courtright, though, and that counts for something.
He's done a lot of brave things."

"And Mrs. Courtright?" she asked. "You mentioned a wife
who was a . . . a gunfighter?"

"She works at Ella Blackwell's Shooting Gallery," I said, "so
she can take care of their children. I think the oldest girl is about
my age, but they live over on Second Street, not in the Acre." As
I said that, it occurred me to that Longhair Jim hadn't been in too
big a hurry yesterday to see his family, and I thought that
strange.

"Then he's a family man," Sallie said. "I'm going to go meet
him," she added casually, and nearly knocked me off my chair,
she surprised me so.

"Why?"

"Curiosity. I don't expect to think much of him. In fact, I took
a strong dislike to him yesterday, and I don't expect to change
my mind. But I've never heard a story like that. Back in Tennessee, we had feudin' and fightin', but lawmen were generally
lawmen, and nobody would understand trying a lawman for
murder, let alone turning out to protect him like that. I don't

know if this place is different . . . or that man is, but I'd be curious to find out."

First Lulabelle predicted that Longhair Jim was trouble, and now Sallie was talking about disliking him. I couldn't understand it. "Probably he really could help find out who killed your cousin," I said a little defensively. "He was an awful good marshal; most everybody was scared of him that ought to be."

"Lizzie, what a wonderful idea! You've just given me the reason to meet him." She threw back her head and laughed, that deep kind of laugh that was so different from any lady's laugh I'd ever heard before. Then she bustled around, folding her mending and clearing up the table, all the while singing something about a highland laddie who was gone.

"And it's oh, in my heart, I wish him safe at home," she sang, and I thought maybe she should be wishing Longhair Jim was safe at home instead of waiting for her at Peer's House. I was beginning to believe that Sallie sang not just from joy but sometimes to help her puzzle things out. I wished singing would help me, for I was puzzled about why Longhair Jim was beginning to change before my very eyes, and why she was going to meet him. Nobody had ever taught me to sing . . . but instinct had taught me to smell trouble coming, and I smelled it now. Sallie didn't have any instinct, as far as I could tell.

"We'll walk back to town together," she said. "I'll be ready in just a minute." And she left the room, singing about that laddie who'd gone to fight for King George upon the throne.

On our way to Peer's House, she mentioned casually that she'd sent a message to Mr. Lambreth, the attorney for her late cousin, that she wished to call about her cousin's business. "Since I'm the only living heir, I'll have to know how the business is running, if it's in debt, and things like that."

"It's like Ben Boy said," I told her. "He was rich, real rich."

"Well, I'll find out tomorrow."

We parted at the door to Peer's House, though curiosity about pushed me right through the doors and into that stuffy plush

lobby. Longhair Jim came to hold the door open for her and
glower at me, so I turned to leave, feeling a little resentful.

"Lizzie?" Sallie called. "Can you be at Mrs. Straight's tomorrow
at noon?"

"Yes, ma'am," I said.

Ben Boy arrived with a whole sack of apples that night, and I
contrived a cobbler, or what passed for cobbler, that I made in
the kettle we hung over a fire just outside the shack. Someone—
his face now long gone from the Acre—had helped us rig a
frame, and we'd found the kettle somewhere. It was the only
place we had to cook.

Ben Boy had probably gotten the apples, one at a time, from a
merchant who'd stored them since they came down from Arkansas in the fall. Farmers up north sent carts to Fort Worth, loaded
with apples. The carts themselves were almost as tempting as
the apples, painted bright red and green, decorated with curli-
cues and canopies, and always pulled by the finest pairs of
matched Thoroughbreds. When the apples were all sold, then
the carts were sold. By then, the horses had paraded through the
city for several days, and there was always a well-to-do busi-
nessman, or one that liked to pretend he was well-to-do, who
would pay handsomely for those fine horses. Ben Boy told me
that selling the horses was the real reason that the carts came
down from Arkansas and that the apples were just a gimmick,
but I refused to believe it. For us, the carts had been created
specially to carry apples so that we could filch them one at a
time when no one was looking. But by February, the apples had
been stored in some merchant's cellar and put out, on sunny
days, in stands in front of the store. Easy pickin' for Ben Boy.

Ben Boy borrowed some fresh milk from somebody's cow—I
never asked but just watched him disappear with the bucket and
return a while later with it half full of milk—and I poured it over
the cobbler when I took it from the fire. It was one of the best
suppers we'd had in weeks, and even July laughed and shouted
when two dogs got into a tug of war over a scrap of garbage.

The air was crisp and cool, and late at night we wrapped our worn blankets around our shoulders and sat outside the shack, staring at the stars. Was there ever, I wondered, such a perfect place? For just a moment I was so secure in my own world that I forgot all about rose-covered fences and soft quilts on real beds.

By noon the next day, I was bursting with curiosity about Sallie's visits with Jim Courtright and that Mr. Lamberth or whatever his name was. But my walk to Mrs. Straight's was slower than usual, because Ben Boy got away without July, and she cried so when I mentioned leaving her alone that I lost heart.

"Come on," I said roughly, grabbing her hand and starting off at a good pace. Of course, it wasn't long before she lagged behind, crying and complaining she was tired, and I had to put her on my back. That slowed us down a whole lot, and tired me out besides. Walking with July in Fort Worth was always somewhat of a trial anyway, and I understood why Ben Boy hated to take her to town. Sometimes folks pointed, and kids yelled out to me, "Hey, you her nanny?" and "Is your momma black or white?" I was capable of telling those kids what to do and where to go in language I'd learned in the Acre, but it always frightened July and made her that much more trouble to hurry along. This day it was a bunch of freighters, standing in front of the wagon yards. They laughed and hoorawed about "that salt and pepper mixture," and while I ignored them, July began to cry and carry on. We arrived at Mrs. Straight's tired and dirty, and I was out of sorts to boot.

"Poor lamb," Nellie Straight cooed. "Come to me," and she held her arms out to July. Mrs. Straight was one of the few persons July trusted since she'd gone with me when I cleaned, and she went without question to sit on that tiny lap and eat warm bread. "You help yourself, Lizzie," Mrs. Straight said, never looking up from July, and that put me further out of sorts.

Sallie watched silently, but something in her eye told me she knew exactly what I felt. "Lizzie," she said, "you take some time and rest a bit, and then let's go for a long walk. I want to go someplace called Samuels Avenue. Do you know where it is?"

How dumb did she think I was? Samuels Avenue led down to the crossing, where the drovers took the cattle across the Trinity River and where old Mr. Satterlee had a raft that you could ride in high water. I'd never had the nickel to spare to ride it, but I wanted to. I wanted to know what it was like not to have firm ground under your feet. "Yeah, I know."

She shot me a look I didn't understand. It was a long time before I learned to say "Yes, ma'am," every time, instead of "Yeah."

"We'll walk down Samuels Avenue," she said, as though the matter was settled, and I guess it was.

A cool glass of buttermilk and a leftover slice of meat pie made me feel lots better. Mrs. Straight had given July some old toys she dug out of heaven knows where, and the ungrateful child didn't even look up when we left.

"Take your time," Mrs. Straight called out. "We'll be just fine."

Three

WE STARTED WALKING, at Sallie's usual good clip, and her singing one of her songs under her breath rather than telling me all about Longhair Jim and the lawyer. I walked along beside her, looking sideways at her every once in a while, and once even coughing a little.

"Catching cold, Lizzie?" It was a cold, blue winter day, and rain spit at us as we walked along dusty streets which were about to turn to mud. I hoped it wouldn't come a norther before we got back.

"No, ma'am. . . . Uh, Miz Sallie, were you . . ." I didn't exactly want to be forward, but I figured it was my business to know. Well, sort of. "Oh, hell, were you going to tell me about Longhair Jim?" The Acre language had slipped out in my frustration.

She whirled on me. "Lizzie Jones, I'll not tell you a thing if I ever hear you talk like that again. A lady does not curse." She pulled her shawl higher on her shoulders, looked straight ahead, and commenced to sing again.

"Yes, ma'am." We walked in silence, and I figured now I never would know.

"He wants to solve my cousin's murder for me," she finally said, and then her face crumpled into laughter. "He says it all has to do with gambling, and he dropped dark hints about lots of money involved. Can you imagine, Lizzie? A McNutt involved in gambling! My poor husband must be spinning in his grave."

It sounded possible to me, and I didn't know why she was laughing so. "What did you tell him?"

"That I had no money to pay him and couldn't hire him. But then he said he was so concerned to clean up the gambling in this city that he'd take the case on without a fee. Something about reopening his detective agency and not being busy."

"If anybody knows about gambling and gamblers, Longhair Jim should," I muttered.

"Why do you say that?" She looked at me with surprise.

"Oh, just rumors that went around before he left, about him looking the other way about crooked games. Some folks thought he took bribe money."

"I expect he might have," she mused. "He's that kind of . . . well, I can't put my finger on it. But I don't trust him. Anyway, I can't stop him from his so-called detecting, but I don't have to be part of it."

I hoped she was right, but I thought maybe she was taking too simple a view of things. If Longhair Jim got to investigating her cousin's murder, she'd be linked with him, willing or not. And once in Fort Worth that would have helped her, but I was beginning to doubt that was still true. I thought Longhair Jim was exciting 'cause of all the things he'd done—like escaping from the Texas Rangers—but if Lulabelle thought he was trouble and Sallie distrusted him, what did other folks in town think? I didn't want to admit it about my hero, but Longhair Jim was maybe on a downhill slide. And I didn't see any reason to let him take Sallie with him on that slide.

We had turned down the bluff on Samuels Avenue, and I still didn't know why we were going this way. Sallie apparently had a habit of doing things her way without explaining to anybody. When we reached Pioneer Rest Cemetery, I thought I knew where we were headed. Mr. McNutt was probably buried there, and she wanted to visit the gravesite. But she walked right on by.

"Uh, don't you . . . I mean . . ." Why was she going down the bluff toward the river?

"Lizzie, we're going to have to teach you to speak up clearly and plainly . . . and without cursing."

"Yes, ma'am. Don't you want to go here to the cemetery?"

"The cemetery? Why?"

"I 'spect this is where Mr. McNutt is buried."

"Oh, really? Yes, let's do go look."

It wasn't all that big a cemetery, and after looking awhile we found a nice big white marble marker with angels on top of it and the words "Stephen McNutt, 1841–1885, Rest in Peace." There was an iron fence all around the grave and fresh flowers on the headstone, but that one mound in there looked kind of lonely.

"Wonder who put the flowers there?" she mused. "He never married. Mr. Courtright talked about that, too. Seemed to think there were dark secrets in his personal life as well as his business matters. Of course, I never knew him, but my husband recalled him as an ordinary man, not one, I don't think, to be involved in all that this Longhair person is hinting about."

We had stopped to sit and rest on a curbing near the grave, huddling next to each other to ward off the drizzling rain.

"Who bought the headstone?" I asked.

"Probably Mr. Lambreth arranged for it," she said. "Maybe he put the flowers there, too. But there's another puzzle."

Lambreth, it seemed, had told her that Mr. McNutt had little or no money, there would be nothing for her to inherit, and she should go on back to Tennessee. He'd notify her when Judd Ambrose was caught and would send her whatever was left from Mr. McNutt's estate after legal fees and the payment of McNutt's debts and so on.

From what Sallie said, Mr. Lambreth was very surprised at her arrival in town. She mimicked him, " 'If only Stephen had mentioned your coming, I could have saved you the wearisome trip out here, only to have to turn around and leave.' I told him I was considering opening the store, and he was horrified. Said I could not legally open the store until the murder was solved.

Nor have possession of Stephen McNutt's house, though he said that was nearly falling down.

"I don't trust him," she said. "Funny, isn't it, how you get a strange feeling when things aren't quite right."

She started that humming again, and I sat as patient as I could, squirming a little now and then. I knew she was figuring on something, with the song helping her think. Finally, as though we hadn't talked about murder and fortunes and dark secrets, she said casually, "This is a pretty cemetery. Is it the only one in town?"

I told her no, but it was the oldest and if we looked we could see the grave of Captain Arnold, who founded the city and was shot by some doctor down south somewhere, and his two babies who died while the Arnolds lived here, and other people from the city's past. Mrs. Straight had brought me here one time, said I needed to know about the past, and told me about the graves and the history of the city. I didn't remember all that much of it, but somehow it fascinated me to think of people who had come here fifty years ago when there wasn't nothing but the bluff and the prairie below and Indians. Fifty years . . . or forty-seven, to be exact, ain't such a long time, but it sure had changed.

"Well," Sallie said, standing up and brushing off her skirt, "we best be going if we're going to see Mr. McNutt's house." So that was it.

"His house?"

"Yes. Mr. Courtright told me it's down on Samuels Avenue, right by the cattle crossing. Said it was pretty grand, but when I asked Mr. Lambreth, he said it was in very poor repair and probably couldn't be sold for enough to fix it up. So I want to see for myself."

We walked fast again until we came to a large, two-story house with a picket fence around the yard and a sign on the fence proclaiming McNUTT. The white paint on the house gleamed, the roof was solid, the yard fairly neat, considering it was winter and all. Behind the house were two outbuildings, both painted and solid-looking.

"In need of repair?" I asked.

"Yes," she laughed. "Seems Mr. Lambreth has some answering to do . . . or maybe I'll just wait and see what he does next. Not tell him I looked at the house."

Sometimes I couldn't follow what she was thinking.

"Let's knock," Sallie said and walked up the stairs bold as you please. I waited at the gate, not exactly afraid mind you but remembering hard-learned lessons about getting caught trespassing. Sallie's knocking brought no response, and she shielded her eyes with her hand, trying to peer in the windows.

"Lizzie," she called. "Come look. The furniture is grand— looks like mahogany. And there are oriental rugs, and beautiful wainscoting." She went from window to window on the verandah, peering in and exclaiming about how grand the house was. I followed more cautiously, but my first peek took my breath away. I never even knew that folks lived in houses like that. There were beautiful vases on the tables and fine paintings on the walls. Mr. McNutt had really been rich!

Finally, Sallie said, "We best get back. Your little friend will be missing you." I was so puzzled by all that Sallie had said that I'd forgotten all about July and probably would have gone back to the Acre without her.

"Yeah," I said.

"Yes, ma'am," she said, and I blushed.

We began walking. "Miz Sallie . . ."

That deep laugh again. "Please, Lizzie, just call me Sallie. Miz Sallie makes me sound like the housekeeper . . . or your grandmother."

"Yes, ma'am. Well, what I meant was . . . I don't understand all this. Mr. Courtright thinks gamblers had something to do with the murder, and Mr. Lambreth says Mr. McNutt was poor, yet there's that big house with all that expensive furniture in it. And maybe Mr. McNutt just ran a store, like everyone thought he did, and then maybe he was a whole different kind of person."

"That's about it, Lizzie. I don't know what to think. But I know what I won't do."

"What?"

"Go back to Tennessee as Mr. Lambreth wants. I considered it yesterday, and then Mr. Courtright's wild tales made me suspicious enough that I was undecided. Now I'm certain I won't go until this is all solved. I feel an obligation to the McNutt family name to see Stephen's murderer apprehended and the mystery of his finances cleared up."

It was near late afternoon by the time we got back to Belknap Street. July was eating fresh sugar cookies, drinking buttermilk, and looking smug.

"I don't wanna go home with you, Lizzie," she said.

I raised my hand to cuff her one, but Nellie Straight stopped me. "Nonsense, July, you'll do as you're told and go home with Lizzie. If you don't make a fuss today, you can come back soon." The stern voice was familiar to me. I'd heard it when my cleaning hadn't quite come up to the mark or when I'd complained about Ma or done something else Nellie didn't like.

July began to wail, great tears streaming down her face. But I was on to her tricks, and I saw her glance at Sallie once or twice to see how her act was being received.

"It is a shame to send the poor thing back to that awful place," Sallie began. "I wish . . . well, never mind."

July stopped crying and looked at Sallie as though to say, "Well, go on, you wish what?"

Sallie finished the sentence lamely herself, "Oh, nothing. I just wish both of you girls lived here. Now, enough of that." And she stood up briskly, as though through with daydreams.

Nellie was not through with the thought though. "They belong in the Acre, and everybody best realize it now. Can't be filling their heads with notions." Nellie was not hard-hearted, just a practical realist, and I knew it. July would never fit in on Belknap Street, where I might could get by, if I learned some manners. But I couldn't, or wouldn't, leave July alone in the Acre. So the whole thing was impossible. It never occurred to me to mourn because I was stuck in the Acre—for life, it looked like. Just as long as I didn't end up in Lulabelle's house.

When I packed July up, clutching a napkin full of cookies and a small rag doll that Nellie had given her, we said our goodbyes. "I'll walk to the corner with you," Sallie said, and I nodded. But Nellie had barely closed the door behind us when it turned out she wanted to ask a question.

"Mrs. Straight," she began, "how did you get to know her? You . . . well, you live in another part of town and . . ."

"The wrong part," I said harshly. "I know I don't belong over here. But Mrs. Straight, she's good to me, lets me do odd jobs for her and lets me be. Doesn't try to change me." That wasn't exactly true, but it sounded good at the time. Nellie Straight didn't allow cursing either. Then I realized I hadn't answered the question.

"Lula . . ." I began and then stopped, at a loss for ways to explain Lulabelle. I tried again. "A lady in the Acre sent me here once on an errand, been a year or more now. She and Mrs. Straight used to know each other, she said, lots of years ago. I never did know the message, but Mrs. Straight started giving me jobs too."

Sallie looked thoughtful. "I think I like your Mrs. Straight very much. Well, I must head back. You girls be careful."

Turned out she was the one who should have been careful. We turned the corner and headed down Rusk Street toward the Acre, but we hadn't gone more than ten feet when I heard Sallie yell indignantly, "You come back here!"

The store on the corner blocked my view, so I couldn't tell why or at who she was yelling. Leaving July, I sprinted around the building and discovered Sallie chasing a boy about my age. He was nearly out of sight around the far corner, clutching the bag he'd grabbed from Sallie. One look told me the whole story.

"Chance Coker," I bellowed, "you bring that back here *now.*"

Chance stopped dead in his tracks at my voice, and then turned around and headed slowly toward us. "Lizzie, keep out of my way," he said angrily, but still he came back. He wouldn't cross me, any more than I would have turned him over to Long-hair Jim.

"She's a friend of mine," I said.

"Well," Chance whined, "how was I supposed to know that?"

Sallie stood staring angrily and managed a deep, sarcastic "Thank you" when he handed back her bag. Then as though he weren't standing right there, she said to me, "He bumped into me hard, nearly knocked me down, and when I got my balance back, he had my bag."

It was Chance's favorite trick, and even I had occasionally feasted on penny candies or some other treat he'd bought with the proceeds. Still, Chance was not among my favorites in the Acre. I didn't trust him, and I didn't like pickpockets, though I usually managed to turn my head at some other less than honorable ways of getting food and money.

Sallie was still puzzled. "He's a friend of yours?"

"Well, sort of," I mumbled.

That made Chance mad. "What do you mean sort of? I gave it back because of you, didn't I?"

People walked by us, curious, but none stopped. Sallie could have needed help—they had no way of knowing—but the safest course was not to get involved, especially with Acre brats, and most people preferred safe. July was looking for safety, too. She had crept around the corner and taken her usual position at the back of my skirt.

"Chance," I said, "you're gonna have to learn that grabbing ladies' bags is dangerous. You'll get caught one day and put on a train out of town."

"Naw," he said. "You just watch, smartie Lizzie. Now I'm sorry I gave it back."

Sallie clutched her bag tighter, but Chance just turned on his heel and left.

"July and I will walk you back to Mrs. Straight's," I said. "But Chance won't be back."

"Don't his parents know what he does?" Sallie asked.

When, I wondered, would she learn that those of us who

grew up in the Acre had neither parents nor family nor watch-dogs? "He ain't got no parents," I said gruffly.

"What happened to them? Where did he come from?" She was full of a thousand questions, and I was getting disgusted.

"I don't know," I said impatiently. "He's just there. Like Ben Boy. Like lots of others." Then, by way of explanation, I added, "I think he's a snowbird."

"Snowbird?"

"Came here to get away from the winters up north. Lots of kids do that, now that they can hide on a train and get here. Sometimes they just put kids on trains back east, knowing they'll get off somewhere in the West."

She was clearly disturbed. "And then they snatch purses?"

"Ben Boy shines shoes," I said indignantly. "And sometimes I sell ribbons or run errands or work for Mrs. Straight. Not every-body's like Chance."

We were back at Mrs. Straight's, and Sallie just kind of drifted away, not really saying goodbye and for sure not saying any-thing about my coming to help her find her way about or some-thing. I figured she was so disgusted with Acre brats that she never wanted to see me again.

Next morning, I was sweeping out the shack while July played with the little doll that Nellie Straight had let her have when Chance Coker walked in big as you please, with a bag of potatoes in his hand.

"Here, Lizzie, I brought you a present."

"Chance Coker, you ain't got no more sense . . ."

"Come on, Lizzie, I'm sorry. I wouldn't have done it if I'd of knowed she was your friend."

"You ought not do it anyway. Filching apples and potatoes"—I pointed to his peace offering—"is one thing. But pickin' pock-ets and snatchin' purses is another, and it's gonna get you caught someday."

"Not me. I'm too fast." He strutted as he said it. "And too smart to spend my days polishing other men's shoes. You gonna boil those potatoes tonight?"

"Yeah. You can come eat if you want."

"Say, I hear your friend is going to investigate her cousin's murder. Seems Longhair Jim thinks there's gambling people involved."

"I already know that," I said loftily, though I was again amazed at Fort Worth's grapevine. Nothing stayed secret for long.

"Well, maybe she's coming down here looking for Jim. I passed her a ways back, headed this direction."

Sallie? Headed for the Acre? One thing I really didn't want was for her to see how and where we lived, the little shack with two rickety chairs, a couple of crates, and an old table that I'd dragged home when someone threw it out. We had one isinglass window, with a bright pretty curtain in it. Ben Boy brought it and I never asked where he got it. Three lean pallets in one corner were our bedroom. No, I didn't want Sallie to see this. I wasn't ashamed, not exactly anyway, but I figured Sallie's seeing the shack would just raise questions—and problems. A big believer in not rocking boats, I couldn't see that Sallie could make life any better for us, and I wasn't ready to take any risks on the off chance that she could. Life had taught me not to expect much.

"Go on, Chance Coker. Just get out of here right now."

As he left, I decided he'd probably made the whole thing up anyway. Sallie wouldn't come to the Acre. I began to pick over the potatoes to see if any were rotten—it was a lot easier to steal old things that the merchants put aside than it was to take the freshest and the newest.

"Lizzie? Lizzie? You got to come to see Miz Lulabelle right now." It was Sophronia, pounding on the wall of the shack.

"What's the matter?"

"There's a lady in the house what's looking for you. Miz Lulabelle says for you to come."

I wasn't sure why, but the idea of Sallie, all practicality and manners and singing her ballads, talking to Lulabelle, with her flowing gowns and all that paint, struck me as the funniest thing

I'd heard in a long time. I laughed aloud, which alarmed both Sophronia and July.

"Come on, July," I said, holding out my hand. "Let's go see what's happening."

If I expected Sallie to be frostily polite or Lulabelle to be nervous and embarrassed, I was in for a big disappointment. When I got to the parlor, the two of them were having a grand visit, drinking coffee and swapping stories. Sallie wore one of her plain gray dresses with a lace jabot at the collar and looked totally out of place in that parlor with its red couches and flowered carpet and mirrors everywhere. Lulabelle, on the other hand, wore one of her outlandish creations and looked like part of the furniture. I could see Maudie Wingo and someone else pushing a swinging door open just a crack so they could peek in and yet not be seen.

"Good morning, Lizzie. Mrs. Brown here—"

"Browning," Lulabelle interrupted. Then, with a giggle, she added, "You know, like the poet lady. But you can call me Lulabelle. Everybody does." And she laughed again, as though it were slightly funny.

"Browning, ah, Lulabelle was just telling me the errands and all you do for her, and I was telling her my wish to take in sewing. We thought you could bring her mending to me, and when it was finished, I could send it back by you. Would you mind? At a quarter a trip?"

"No, ma'am." For some reason, the idea made me nervous. I think I didn't like the link between my two worlds, between Sallie, who represented possibilities, and the Acre, which was reality.

"We've been having a wonderful time," Lulabelle said. "I was telling Sallie how sad we all were at the death of her cousin, Mr. McNutt, but she says she has help in straightening out his affairs and finding the wretch that done him in."

"Longhair Jim," I volunteered.

That stopped even Lulabelle for a moment. "You don't mean . . . ?"

"Yeah, Longhair Jim wants to help her solve the murder." I didn't see why Lulabelle had to act so surprised. He *was* a detective, after all.

But Lulabelle turned solemn, just like she had the last time I'd mentioned Longhair Jim. "You watch out for that one, miss. There's no good ever comes when he's around."

Sallie said, "Yes, ma'am," in a proper tone and threw me a look to remind me I'd said "Yeah" again. Then she went on, "There are some very peculiar circumstances, Mrs. Browning." I guess she just wasn't comfortable calling her Lulabelle. "And some conflicting stories. I'd appreciate it if you'd keep an ear open for anything you might hear."

"Well, of course I will. I do hear about most everything that happens, sooner or later. I didn't happen to know Mr. McNutt" —Sallie raised her eyebrows at that—"but I understand he was a fine and honest gentleman. A shame, just a shame." Lulabelle began to wring her hands.

Sallie started to take her leave, thanking Lulabelle for her courtesy and all that. But then just as she was at the door, with July and me on her heels, she turned to Lulabelle. "I do worry about these children," she said, nodding at us.

Lulabelle was so used to us that I guess it never occurred to her to worry. "You do?" she said, in a surprised tone.

"Yes, I do," Sallie said firmly. "They'll have no future unless we change their present circumstances."

"I told Lizzie it was about time she thought about working—" Lulabelle never got to finish that sentence.

"That's not what I had in mind, Mrs. Browning. Good day." And we were out on the street.

"Lizzie," Sallie asked angrily, "what kind of a city have I come to? Murders being covered up, children living on the streets, and no one seems to care."

I didn't know what to say. Life in the Acre was just what it was, and I had no standard of comparison. Sallie, coming from some other place, apparently knew something different and better, and I envied her that. But it had never occurred to me to envy before, not even well-dressed and well-fed youngsters from across town who slept soundly in soft feather beds every night. I just accepted that some of us, myself included, were "have-nots." Sallie made me think, and she made me less reluctant to show her the shack. It was what I had, and I did the best I could with it.

"Come on, July," I said. "Let's show Sallie where we live."

I got to give her credit. Sallie never did exclaim over how bare the shack was or how cold it must be in winter or any of its other faults. She looked around a long time without saying anything, her eyes taking in the bare pallets, the bright curtain, the few chipped dishes. And then she said, "Your mother doesn't live here, does she, Lizzie?"

"No, ma'am. I . . . I didn't know how to tell you that."

"Oh, dear heaven," she muttered, then louder, to me, "And you keep house here, don't you?"

"Somebody's got to feed July and Ben Boy," I said defensively. "I don't do no more than I have to."

"Any more," she said absently. "Yes, you do, Lizzie. You could walk away and let them be by themselves, but you don't. Who owns this awful place . . . sorry, I mean this . . ."

I laughed at her then. "Shack? It's pretty awful, and I know it. But I don't know who owns it. Maybe Lulabelle, for all I know. It was empty and we started sleeping in it, and nobody ever said nothing to us."

"Anything to us."

I felt I had to add, "Lulabelle watches out for us, gives us food now and again."

"How kind of her!" I thought I heard sarcasm in her voice, but then, more seriously, she went on, "Lizzie, I make you a promise. I'm going to get you three out of the Acre. You and July and Ben Boy, even though I don't know him."

The thought scared me. The Acre was home, all I'd ever known, and I wasn't at all sure I wanted to leave it, in spite of the daydreams that Nellie Straight's house inspired. Oh, sure, like everybody I thought I wanted to see the elephant—that's what the cowboys that came through town called it when they headed north up the trail to see all the sights of the world beyond Texas. July still thought there was a real elephant at the end of the trail somewhere, and I'd given up explaining it to her. Yeah, I wanted to see the elephant, but I think I wanted the elephant to come to the Acre.

Sometimes you don't recognize what's right in front of you. Sallie was bringing the elephant to the Acre.

Four

WHEN SHE LEFT the Acre, Sallie had asked me to come to Mrs. Straight's by noon the next day, but I never did make it because that was the day I found Dickey-bird and added him to our family in the shack, as if we needed one more mouth to feed. About Ben's age but thin and pale, he stood huddled against a storefront, hands shoved in his pockets and coat collar turned up to his ears. An old ragged scarf around his neck did little to keep him warm, and the funny hat on his head probably didn't do much either. I started to walk by but the look on his face stopped me. It wasn't fright like July, or hunger, or self-pity. It was more like resignation.

"You new here?" I challenged.

"Yeah." The voice was still high and squeaky, even though he spoke so softly I could barely hear him.

"Where'd you come from?"

"North."

"North where?"

"Illinois. Pa brought me."

"Where's your pa now?"

"He rode out. Said for me to take care of myself, he'd be back in a couple of months."

"Where's your ma?"

The look changed to sadness, and I thought I saw a tear. "She died last year."

I hoped there hadn't been any tears, because crying was

something no Acre brat did. July was too young to make such fine distinctions, though, and she looked solemnly at him, then went quietly over and put her hand on his arm.

"My ma died too," she told him.

He pulled a hand out of its pocket and took hers, and I knew there would be no separating them.

"You best come with us," I said flatly. "What's your name?"

"Dickey."

"Dickey-bird," laughed July, and the name stuck.

"Yes, we'll call you Dickey-bird because you're a snowbird from up north," I said. "Come along now, you two." At least with Dickey to hold her hand, July wouldn't fuss for me to pick her up. I walked fast, occasionally calling to them to hurry up. When we walked by an apple cart, I filched two and put them in the sack I always carried, and when we passed Mrs. German's house, I snuck in to pull one of her winter onions.

Ben Boy was a little put out when he saw Dickey-bird. "Who's that?" he asked, not bothering to whisper.

"Dickey-bird. I found him on the street in town today. His pa left him here and went on." None of us found that story preposterous, because we had no reason to associate parents and responsibility.

"Dickey-bird," Ben Boy echoed. "What kind of a name is that?"

"It's a pretty name," July said defensively, grabbing her new hero by the hand.

"We gonna feed him?" Ben Boy asked with practicality.

"He'll earn his keep," I said, as much to Dickey-bird as to Ben Boy. "Maybe he can shine shoes with you."

"Don't need nobody else takin' work I can do." Ben Boy folded his arms and looked ready to fight. "But I hear tell Uncle Billy needs somebody to swamp out the saloon mornings."

I hesitated just a minute. Whoever swamped out Uncle Billy's so-called cattle exchange was liable to have to swamp out drunks left from the night before. Dickey-bird looked a little frail and inexperienced for the work. But why was I protecting him?

Part of our code in the Acre was that everyone had to learn to take care of himself, no matter what.

"Sure," I said. "I'll take him over in the morning."

That seemed to mollify Ben Boy. Later on I caught him talking to Dickey-bird off in a corner, and I sensed he was giving him a few pointers. It wouldn't hurt Ben Boy at all to have someone look up to him. But it struck me that what Ben Boy would teach him would not be all honest, and that was too bad. It would make Sallie ask again what kind of a city she had come to. And then I wondered why I thought of that.

We had a party that night, sort of, to welcome Dickey-bird. Sophronia gave me some tough old beef, and I made a stew-soup out of it with Mrs. German's onion, and we had apples for dessert. Ben Boy went and got fresh milk and produced some penny candies from somewhere.

"This is fun," said Dickey-bird. "It's like camping out."

"Yeah," I said, "just like camping out. Where'd your pa go, Dickey-bird?"

"I dunno. He just said he had to go on, and I should stand on a corner until somebody came and helped me. Said he'd come back, though, and he probably will."

"Lucky it weren't no hide hunter that came to help you," Ben Boy said. "You'd be out to Buffalo Gap cooking and cleaning up in the smelliest camp you ever saw."

"I wouldn't have gone," Dickey said indignantly.

"Might not have had a choice," Ben Boy said darkly, managing to scare our newcomer thoroughly.

"Ben Boy just means you best be careful around some folks here, and never look like you're lost—like you looked when I found you," I told him.

"I'm glad you found me," he said contentedly, and I knew he hadn't realized what kind of a world he'd landed in.

Chance barged into the shack a little later that night, shouting about a big fight at the dance hall. "Called the marshal and everything," he said. "You ought to go see. Started when two of them dance hall girls got into it. Both wanted to dance with the

same man. They went after each other with beer bottles, and it
wasn't long before everyone took sides. It was a holy mess!" He
rubbed his hands gleefully, and then he noticed Dickey-bird
cowering in the corner. "Who the hell's that?"

Now I was resolved not to defend Dickey-bird, and I didn't
object to Chance swearing even though Sallie made me careful
about it myself, but Chance made me mad. The shack was our
home, and he had no right to come barging in and be ugly
about someone we had invited in. I walked toward him with my
hands on my hips. "His name's Dickey-bird, and he lives here," I
said in my firmest tone. But I knew instantly I made a mistake.

"Dickey-bird?" Chance was convulsed with laughter. "Looks
like a bird." And he laughed uproariously at his own humor.

Poor Dickey-bird cowered even farther into the corner, and
July went over to put her hand in his again. "Don't listen to
him," she said. "Chance is mean." And she stuck her tongue out
at him.

"Don't you stick your tongue out at me, brat," Chance
warned, advancing toward her.

July lost all her bravery and darted for my skirts. Pushing her
aside, I reached for the broom and swung it in a wide arc, barely
missing Chance. Ben Boy was almost an accidental victim of my
anger, but he managed to dodge out of the way.

"Chance Coker, you get out of here," I warned, raising the
broom again.

"You can't make me," he taunted, but he edged toward the
door. "I was just going anyway. And you see, Lizzie Jones, if I
ever do anything for you again." He disappeared into the night.

"He's all bluff," I assured Dickey. "He won't hurt you. He
don't dare, 'cause he's afraid of me." Satisfied, I stood my broom
back up against the wall. But then I very solemnly announced
that Dickey-bird had a new name, as of that moment. "We will
call him Richard," I said.

"He's my Dickey-bird," July wailed, running to him.

I knew he'd be Dickey-bird forever. We made room for him
on our pallets that night, and the poor thing slept soundly, no

doubt worn out by his day. July curled against him, as though I'd never done a thing for her.

Next morning, before I could even take Dickey-bird to Billy Winder's to see about swamping, Ben Boy came running back to the shack.

"Thought you was off shining shoes," I said crossly as he burst in yelling my name.

"I was," he said indignantly, "and somebody else'll probably get all the good ones, now that I'm back here." He paused for breath. "But that lady—Miz McNutt—she found me and paid me a quarter to come get you. Said she was real worried 'cause you didn't show up yesterday."

Worried? Over me? It was a new thought. "Well, I couldn't," I said crossly, " 'cause of Dickey-bird."

"Don't tell me," Ben Boy said, "go tell her. She wants you to come right away, says it's important."

So I went quick to take Dickey-bird to Uncle Billy Winder. 'Course he weren't nobody's uncle, but everyone called him that, even Lulabelle. She and Uncle Billy didn't talk much, though—there was bad feelings between them such as I never understood.

"Lord, Lizzie, what're you doin' wakin' a man in the middle of the night?" He peered at me through puffy eyes, pulling a suspender over his shoulder with one hand and trying to open the door with the other.

"It's morning, Uncle Billy. And the sun is shining."

He blinked hard. "So it is. Damn bright, isn't it? Cold, too." He shivered and folded his arms as though to hold in his own warmth.

"Uncle Billy, this here's Richard. I hear you need someone to swamp for you. He needs a job."

Uncle Billy focused his eyes on Dickey-bird, who stood beside me stiff as a ramrod, his hands in front of him clasping that funny cap. "Richard, huh? Ain't seen you before. You new?"

"Yessir."

"Look kind of puny to me. Sure you can swamp?"

Dickey-bird didn't look as though he were sure of a thing in this world, but I said firmly, " 'Course he can."

"Quarter a day, seven days a week." Uncle Billy scratched and pretended to stare at the sky.

Dickey-bird looked to me for approval, but I said, "No, Uncle Billy. That's plain robbery. Fifty cents a day for hard work."

"Ain't worth it. I'll swamp myself."

I laughed at him. "Call me to come watch."

"Don't get smart with me, Lizzie Jones. Your ma still owes me a tab in here—been a long time on the books now."

"Ma's gone, and that's not my business," I said, wishing she hadn't sat at Uncle Billy's all those nights. But there was nothing to be done about Ma. Dickey-bird I could help. "Well, is it a deal? I got to be goin'."

"I'll give it a trial," Uncle Billy said. "Come on in, uh . . . Richard . . . sure is a funny name . . . I'll show you where the stuff is."

Dickey-bird followed him, throwing a woeful look over his shoulder at me.

Sallie was pacing the floor when July and I got there. "Lord, Lizzie, I was worried about you. Are you all right?"

Having her worry was nice, but I didn't like having to be beholden to someone, having to report. "I was busy," I said.

She almost smiled. "Oh, I see. Busy. Silly me to have thought you might have needed help. Or to have cared."

"Yes, ma'am," I said, "but, uh, thanks." I was embarrassed, uncertain of what to do or say.

"You girls will stay for lunch," Mrs. Straight said, rescuing me by coming into the room.

"Of course they'll stay. I've got plans for Lizzie that may take most of the day," Sallie said. "But I've got to finish mending those two gowns for Mrs. Browning. Lizzie, I made them a little bigger but she'll never know. You must take them back with you. Now, let me finish them and we'll go to work on you."

"Me?"

"Yes, ma'am. We're going to wash your hair and curl it and I've got an old dress I think would fit you better than me."

I hated charity, and I knew enough to realize that nobody came from Tennessee with an old dress they were ready to throw away. "No, ma'am," I said. "I can't take your dress."

"Lizzie Jones, you'll learn soon enough there's a grace to be had about taking as well as giving. Besides, I want to take you someplace with me when I get you fixed up."

"Where?" I asked suspiciously.

"The White Elephant Saloon," she said, calm as you please.

The White Elephant was a high-toned saloon, not like Uncle Billy's or any of the places in the Acre. This was up on Main Street, near the courthouse, and it was where all the swell folks went to drink and gamble. But ladies didn't generally go there alone.

"Why are we goin' to the White Elephant?" I tried to sound as calm as she did.

"To meet Mr. Courtright. He, ah, wants me to see something."

Before too long, I was dressed in a blue flannel dress, the best I'd ever worn, with soft pleats coming down from the tight waist and a high plain collar. My hair was pulled back from my face, with curls falling down on my neck.

"There. Look at yourself," Sallie commanded, holding up a hand mirror. "No, wait, I know just the thing that's missing." And she went to get a lace collar that hung square in the back and tied in the front like a scarf. "Now," she commanded, and I looked.

It was wonderful, of course. I'd never had clothes like that, nor anyone to teach me much to do with my hair, and I felt a little less plain than usual. But it was all wrong, and there was no way I could tell Sallie. I felt like a doll that she'd been dressing, or maybe Cinderella as midnight neared. At the end of the day, I'd have to go back to the Acre and my own drab clothes. It was almost better not to tempt yourself with things if you knew you couldn't keep them.

I pretended to dance around the room, swirling my skirt, to show how pleased I was. But then I remembered about the White Elephant, and my bravado left me. "Do I really have to go with you to meet Longhair Jim?"

"You don't think I'd go to a place like that alone, do you? I feel a little guilty taking a child of your age"—indignantly, I stood taller as she said that—"but I have no choice. You will be my chaperone."

"And I'm going to work on fixing a coat for July while you're gone," Mrs. Straight said. "I've got a trunk of the mister's in the attic that's got some old blankets in it. I think I can cut one into a fine warm coat."

And so that's how we came to leave July with Mrs. Straight and walk to the White Elephant, me protesting all the while and Sallie telling me to hush.

Longhair Jim was waiting near the door when we got there, and he was obviously startled to see someone with Sallie. But the laugh was that he didn't recognize me.

"Miz McNutt, glad you could make it. I think you'll find this instructive. I . . . I wasn't expecting a companion." He looked purposefully in my direction.

"Oh, Mr. Courtright, you remember Lizzie Jones, don't you? She's the one who was there that first day when the coach let me out in the, what do you call it? . . . the Acre."

He looked positively livid then. "Oh, yes. Well, stay here by the door. We'll return shortly."

Ever so gently, Sallie took my arm. "Mr. Courtright, I couldn't leave that child alone in a place like this. She'll come with me. Come along, Lizzie."

"As you wish," he grumbled, leading her away with me trotting along behind, wishing Sallie would not refer to me as a child.

The White Elephant was the grandest place I'd ever seen. Oh, I'd peeked in the door a time or two before but always got run off before I got a good look. Now I could stare at the huge mahogany bar that ran the length of one wall, with ornately

carved decorations on shelves that held row upon row of sparkling glasses. In the center, there was an enormous mirror, and
in front of the bar was a brass railing for gentlemen to rest their
feet on. The floor was covered with a deep rich red carpet and
the doorways were hung with velvet drapes.

I stared so hard I forgot about Longhair Jim and Sallie, and
they got ahead of me. "Come along, Lizzie," Sallie said, coming
back to get me and pulling gently on my arm. We went to a table
off in a corner, and Longhair Jim ordered whisky for himself and
hot tea for us, though he tried his best to get Sallie to have
something he called a cordial.

"Now, Mr. Courtright," Sallie said in a most businesslike tone,
"why are we here?"

That annoyed him, and he looked pained, putting a finger to
his mouth in the old gesture that calls for silence. "The walls
around this place have ears," he whispered.

Sallie lowered her voice and tried again. "But what can we
learn here? Did Stephen spend time in the White Elephant?"

"Probably," he whispered so low that I could barely hear him
and had to strain over the table so as not to miss a word. "There
are games upstairs—faro, keno, what have you—and this is
where the cream of society comes to gamble."

"And what will we learn by being here?"

"For one thing, we'll see who we see. And I thought you
should visit the saloon to begin to get a feel for the way your
cousin lived."

"Do we know that he came here regularly? Or even once in a
while?"

"Well, not exactly," Jim hedged, "but it's probable. I'd say
highly probable."

"I fail to see . . ." Sallie began.

"Ma'am, I'm a detective, and you'll have to trust me in these
matters," he said, kind of puffing out his chest. Longhair Jim
downed his whisky and called for another.

Whatever Sallie was going to say to him was cut off by the
appearance of a short, well-dressed man. "Courtright," he said,

holding out his hand though his voice was cool and not at all cordial, "good to see you back in town."

"Huh, oh, yeah, thanks, Luke." He half rose to shake the man's hand, then sat right back down and looked away. Obviously, he wished this man would go away, but the newcomer didn't.

Of course I knew right away who he was. None other than Luke Short, the famous gambler and shootist. He was as much a legend as Longhair Jim, for it was rumored that he'd run with Bat Masterson and Wyatt Earp up in Kansas until vigilantes ran them off. Short supposedly had killed at least two men in cold blood. Fair fights, yes, but still cold blood. His eyes were green and made him look like the kind of man who could kill in cold blood. But he was handsome—younger than Jim, and better dressed, his suit perfectly free of wrinkles, while Jim looked more rumpled every time I saw him. Reluctantly, I realized that Luke Short was much more in command of the situation than Longhair Jim, and then I began to wonder if he was a faster draw too.

"You aren't going to introduce me," Short said, and it was obvious he was right. "Permit me, ladies; Luke Short at your service."

I just looked at my hands in my lap, not knowing what to do, but Sallie gave him her hand and said, "Sallie McNutt from Tennessee."

"McNutt? Strange, that name's familiar."

"Perhaps you knew my late cousin, Stephen McNutt. He owned McNutt's Mercantile Store."

"That's it," Short said. "No, I didn't know him, but of course I heard of his death. Everyone in town did. Have they found the murderer yet?"

Sallie glanced at Jim. "No, not yet. You're quite certain my cousin did not, ah, come in here?"

"He may have come in for a drink, ma'am, but he never wagered upstairs. Of that I'm certain."

Longhair Jim glowered, and Sallie looked at him as if to say, "Now what?"

All Jim said was, "Short, I've business with you. You'll be around awhile?"

"Anytime, Jim," he said easily. "Ladies, a pleasure to meet you." He actually took Sallie's hand again and bowed low to kiss it. Then he was gone.

"Can't believe a thing that man tells you," Jim muttered. "Of course Stephen McNutt gambled here. Why else would he have had so much money?"

"Maybe he earned it," Sallie suggested.

"You don't earn that kind of money in this town," Jim said confidently. "But don't you worry, I'll keep working on this. I've got to see Short on another matter—law enforcement—and I'll push him some more."

"You do that," Sallie said with a slight grin. "We must be going now."

As Longhair Jim escorted Sallie to the door, with me trailing behind again, I saw Sallie give a startled gasp and then kind of duck her head. She glanced back at me, then across the room again, and then directly at Jim.

"It's been a most informative visit, Mr. Courtright. I do thank you."

And we were soon on the street, headed home. Sallie was obviously preoccupied, so we walked in silence—she didn't even hum under her breath—until she said, "Did you see him?"

"Who?" I asked.

"Mr. Lambreth. He was in that . . . that place. And he was going upstairs. Stephen McNutt may not have wagered, as Mr. Short calls it, but Walter Lambreth does. I think that's something to remember."

Not knowing Mr. Lambreth, I of course hadn't noticed him. But I had seen several businessmen come in as we left, and I supposed he was one of them.

Sallie voiced two opinions as we walked back to Mrs. Straight's. One was that Luke Short was perfectly charming. I groaned but figured I didn't need to tell her about the men he'd killed and the color of his eyes. Her other opinion was that Jim Courtright didn't know what he was doing, and I reluctantly agreed with that, but I didn't tell her so. It's hard to turn your back on a hero.

"He's always boasting how good he is, but I don't see any evidence. He hasn't told us anything about my cousin that we couldn't have figured out ourselves. And did you see him have four drinks this afternoon?" As though she had figured things out to her satisfaction, she began to hum yet another song, and we walked faster, to get in out of the cold wind.

July greeted us wearing a shapeless but warm woolen coat cut from an old army blanket. "See?" she said proudly. "New coat."

"Pretty, July," I said. "Come on now, we have to get back. We best get home while the sun's still out a little bit. I'll just get out of these clothes—"

"Get out of them?" Sallie asked. "No, Lizzie, they're yours to keep."

"I appreciate that, ma'am. But I can't wear them to the Acre. They'd just get ruined . . . or stolen. I'll leave them here. But July can surely wear her new coat." I tried to put a note of enthusiasm into my voice, but it was hardly noticeable, and Sallie looked like a child whose candy had spilled in the dirt.

Dickey-bird was curled up on the pallets sound asleep when July and I got home, and July, with strong mothering instinct, ran to him immediately. She sat beside him, stroking his head and crooning something I couldn't understand, until he began to stir and stretch. Rubbing his eyes with balled fists, he sat up and stared around as though to orient himself.

"I guess . . . I fell asleep when I got through at Uncle Billy's," he said apologetically.

"How was it?" I asked.

"Oh, okay," was the offhand answer, followed in a minute by something closer to the truth. "Mopping floors is hard work."

I laughed, then said preachily, "Hard work won't hurt you."

"There was some old man in there, asleep, in a corner. I just kind of mopped around him. He smelled bad."

"You get your fifty cents?"

"Sure," he said proudly, holding up two quarters.

"Good, we need some bacon for supper. I'll cut it up to flavor the potatoes good."

Dickey-bird looked long and hard at the two quarters, then at me, and then back to the two quarters.

"You can't just keep them, you know," I said in exasperation.

"Yeah, I know. Here." And he reluctantly handed them to me.

"I'll fetch a sweet, too," I said, throwing on my coat to go back out. "You two wait here for Ben Boy."

After that, Dickey-bird's fifty cents bought a daily treat as well as food. Some days he earned more than Ben Boy, but I always thought he worked harder and longer. Shining shoes was good work compared to swamping a saloon.

Five

MR. WALTER LAMBRETH, a fat attorney with a walrus mustache and a big gold watch chain stretched across his middle, came to call on Sallie the very next day. July, Mrs. Straight, and I strained against the parlor door to hear every word he said. We were careful to be quiet, until I got so mad I wanted to yell at him, and Mrs. Straight had to clamp a hand over my mouth.

Mr. Lambreth near lectured Sallie on her having stayed in Texas when she should have gone back to her people in Tennessee.

"I have no people left back there," she told him.

"Well, my dear," he said in a tone that sent distrust through me like lightning, "you have friends, connections there. And you could no doubt find work suited to your skills." He sounded scornful.

"Mr. Lambreth," Sallie said in a direct tone of voice, "I intend to reopen McNutt's Mercantile. I will run the store."

He cleared his throat in alarm. "Of course that's impossible, absolutely impossible. The will cannot be cleared until the murder is solved and that . . ." He shrugged his shoulders, as though to say, "Who knows when?" Then, as though Sallie were a disrespectful child whose words were to be ignored, he changed the subject. "Shall I attempt to sell the house? Of course, in the repair it's in, it won't bring much, but perhaps . . ."

"I think not yet," Sallie told him. "I intend to live in the house. I am the sole heir, is that not true?"

"Well, yes, my dear, though I hardly call it being an heir, poor Stephen had so little left. There's nothing, almost nothing." I could tell he was wringing his hands in pity for Sallie, and I wondered why Sallie didn't tell him she knew the house wasn't in poor repair. We'd seen it, and it was a fine house. But I guessed Sallie had her reasons—and later I found out she surely did.

"Well," she said brightly, "there's the store and the house in whatever shape it's in"—the slight sarcasm in her voice was lost on Mr. Lambreth—"and whatever else is certainly more than I thought I'd have."

"You cannot possibly open the store, even after the estate is cleared. You know nothing about business, the debts . . ."

"Mr. Lambreth, I'd like to open the store tomorrow. If I can't legally own it, surely I can lease it . . . and perhaps thereby I'll make a little money toward paying off Mr. McNutt's debts. He was, after all, a relative who bore my name, and I could not bear to have the family name sullied by unpaid debts."

With that, Sallie swept her hand across her forehead in a dramatic gesture, and I wanted to whisper to her that she was overdoing it. But I was wrong.

Walter Lambreth frowned and scowled and coughed and cleared his throat, but he couldn't seem to get any words out.

"Is there any reason I cannot operate the store temporarily as a paid employee?" Sallie asked innocently. "If need be, I'm sure we could consult a judge for an opinion."

A sound like "harrumph" came from Mr. Lambreth, and then he said, "I'm sure that won't be necessary. But I warn you, Mrs. McNutt, you will make no money, and the estate cannot bear the responsibility for any further debt you incur."

"I'll take that risk," Sallie said confidently. "I'll meet you in front of the store at 9 A.M. in the morning, and I expect you to unlock the premises and turn the keys over to me."

"We'll see, we'll see . . ." He appeared to be thinking her words over, but the next thing she said caught him up short.

"If you feel a legal agreement is necessary," she said sweetly, "I'll consult another lawyer to represent me so that you won't have a conflict of interest."

"You wouldn't dare," he thundered, and then calmed down instantly. "No, no, that won't be necessary. We'll just operate on a verbal agreement."

It struck me, little as I knew, as a funny way for a lawyer to do business, but Sallie just smiled and said, "Fine. I'll see you in the morning."

Defeated, Mr. Lambreth took his leave, muttering something about women with no business sense who refused to rely on good counsel when it was given them.

We almost fell through the door where we'd been listening, and Sallie laughed her deep laugh. "You heard then?"

"Yes, ma'am," I said indignantly. "He sure is in a hurry to get rid of you."

"Isn't he just," she mused, staring absently at me. Suddenly her eyes focused clearly.

"What about the house?" I asked breathlessly, remembering the beautiful furniture and fine rugs.

"That," she said, "will have to wait. Until the store brings in a little profit, I can't afford to open the house. And it can sit there . . . it's not losing money like the store is. Lizzie," she said in a no-nonsense tone, "your dress is spotted with mud. Do see if you can wash it off."

Sallie was standing in the middle of the store when July and I got there around ten the next morning, her hands on her hips, her expression fierce. "Look at this mess," she said. "Not only was the cash register emptied, apparently, but whoever murdered him willfully destroyed merchandise, maybe to make it look like robbery. Mr. Lambreth just locked it up as it was. No wonder he handed me the keys and left immediately. He was probably laughing to himself, the old goat!"

I had never heard her quite so ferocious, but it tickled me to hear her call Lambreth an old goat, and I would have laughed aloud if I hadn't looked around at the store. Piles of clothes, once neatly folded, fell about on the floor and display counters. Sacks of coffee and flour were split, probably with the same knife that murdered Mr. McNutt, and their contents were spilled on the floor. Picture glass was smashed, canned goods flung about, and one beautiful leather saddle had a slash in it.

"Sallie," I said tentatively, "look at this saddle. The slash mark looks brand-new, not like it was done two or three months ago when Mr. McNutt was murdered."

She walked over to where I stood and examined the saddle carefully, rubbing at the cut in the leather with a tentative finger. "You're right, Lizzie, it surely does. I wonder what that means?"

After we'd all prowled around the store for a bit, Sallie said, "We have a week's work here, even to get it ready for customers." And then she put each of us to work, July refolding clothes —she turned out to be very neat and careful about it—and me mopping and dusting, while she tried to sort out the canned goods and basic supplies.

"What in heaven's name are you doing?" Late in the afternoon, a familiar voice boomed from the door, and there stood Longhair Jim, weaving a little and blinking as his eyes adjusted from the sunshine outside to the dark of the store. "You didn't check with me about this!" he accused indignantly.

Sallie, up on a ladder by the top shelf of spices, turned to look at him. "I had no idea that was expected," she said coldly, and I could tell that she was too tired to be very polite.

"What are you doing?" he repeated.

"Getting ready to open the store," Sallie said, turning back to the spices.

"But you can't." He had wandered over to the counter where I was scrubbing preserves off the top, and I could smell whisky on his breath.

"Why can't I?" Sallie kept on working and spoke without looking at him.

"Because . . ." For a moment, I thought he had no idea why she couldn't, but then he said firmly, "Because it's too dangerous."

"I suppose Judd Ambrose will come back to murder me, just as he murdered Stephen?" She wiped her hands on the big apron she wore and started down the ladder. "I really doubt that, Mr. Courtright."

"Jim," he muttered, "call me Jim." Then he spoke more forcefully. "I told you Judd Ambrose didn't do it. And, yes, I think somebody wants this store bad enough to kill again."

"But your assertion has always been that Stephen was killed over gambling debts."

"But not necessarily his own debts," Jim said, which left me puzzled.

Sallie looked puzzled too. "Well, I shall be very careful," she said.

Jim waved a vague hand in the air. "I'll have to be comin' by here all the time now," he said unhappily and turned around and left, still walking a little unsteadily.

"He's been drinking," Sallie said as though I didn't already know.

"Bad man," July said, shaking her head seriously and going back to folding shirts.

Sallie was right. It took us one week to clean and straighten the store, and it was a week of the hardest work I'd ever done. Sallie paid me fifty cents a day, so the four of us—Ben Boy, Dickey-bird, July, and me—ate particularly well. One night I even bought a piece of beef stew meat, better than the tough old pieces Sophronia gave us, and some turnips. It made a hearty stew, though I had to convince Dickey-bird that turnips were *not* poison, no matter what his pa had told him.

I was able to hoard some money away in a secret hiding place, but I came home at night as tired as Dickey-bird after he swamped the saloon, and all of us fell onto our pallets, exhausted. Sallie tried a time or two to get July and me to go to

Mrs. Straight's with her for supper, but I refused. Ben Boy and Dickey-bird wouldn't be much about fixing themselves meals, and besides, Mrs. Straight shouldn't have to feed us, though Lord knows that good woman would have been willing. No, the Acre was home.

The day we changed the CLOSED sign for one that said OPEN, the store sparkled and shone. Neat piles of shirts and pants were stacked on display tables, canned goods lined the shelves, saddles sat on wooden horses, tools hung from the pressed tin ceiling, and Sallie stood by the door waiting. And waiting. By ten o'clock in the morning, not a customer had come in.

"Our sign isn't big enough," she decided. "Nobody knows we're open." She thought a minute, then bustled about getting her cape and saying, "Lizzie, lock the door and keep it locked. Take the sign down for a bit."

Puzzled, I did as she said, and she went to the desk that had been Stephen's and now was hers, and wrote something. Then she headed for the door, calling over her shoulder, "I'll be right back."

We had only three sales all day, and small sales at that. But the next day, people came in like cattle on the trail. "Glad to see you're open," said one man, while another mourned, "Terrible thing about poor McNutt," and still another asked, "Who's in charge here?" and looked incredulous when Sallie said she was. It seemed Sallie had put an ad in the *Daily Democrat* and that was how folks knew the store was open.

At the end of that day, we had sold seven dollars and eighty-five cents worth of goods, and we felt like merchant kings. Once I looked out and saw Walter Lambreth pacing up and down across the street, staring at the customers going into the store. I didn't tell Sallie about it for fear of alarming her, but he gave me the willies.

Once the store was running a little bit smoothly, Sallie busied herself with the books. I waited on customers, most of the time without needing her help, and July folded and straightened, and all the while Sallie had her nose buried in dusty old ledgers at the desk that sat in the back of the store. Finally, after five days, she raised her eyes.

"Stephen McNutt was a rich man," she said.

I wanted to ask her what else was new. We had known all along that he was rich. But I just waited for her to say more.

"These books," she said, "they show a thriving business . . . and accounts due him in the thousands of dollars." Then she looked thoughtful. "And Mr. Lambreth tells me there's no estate."

I was beginning to smell the same rat Sallie was. "Why did he leave the books for you to see?" I asked. "If they show Mr. McNutt was rich, I'd think Mr. Lambreth would have hidden them . . . or changed them."

"Very good, Lizzie," Sallie said. "I'd have thought so too . . . and I think the answer is no compliment to me. He probably thought I couldn't . . . or wouldn't bother . . . to figure them out. But he was wrong."

As far as I could see, two men in Fort Worth were both very wrong about Sallie McNutt.

After that, life settled into a pattern. February wore on, colder than usual, and Ben Boy took to shining shoes inside the Metropolitan when they would let him. Dickey-bird took longer and longer to swamp the saloon, just so he could stay where it was warm.

Ben Boy stopped in the store sometimes, and Dickey-bird once in a while came by after he finished at the saloon, so pretty soon Sallie knew both of them.

One day she announced, "I think we need more help here."

"What for?" I asked. I'd been sitting on my hands most of the morning while she took care of customers, now that her nose was out of the ledgers.

"Well, business has increased," she said. "What about Ben Boy and Dickey?" Somehow she never liked the name Dickey-bird, but every time she called him Dickey, July would interrupt with "Dickey-*bird.*"

"They have jobs," I pointed out.

"But such jobs," Sallie laughed. "Shining shoes out in the cold, and swamping out a smelly old saloon. I want them to work here."

"They don't need no other jobs," I insisted. "They're both doing fine. Dickey-bird gets fifty cents a day."

"I'll pay him fifty cents." She pretended to be studying her ledger book. "Yes, fifty cents."

"To do what?" I asked, swinging down from the counter where I'd perched.

"Deliver," she said firmly.

"I can deliver," I countered. "I'm not doing nothing most of the day."

"It isn't ladylike," she said, closing the subject. Sallie had a knack for getting things her way, and Dickey-bird came to work at the store. He was delighted, because he always hated the saloon and was afraid of the drunks he stumbled over. I'd watched him many a morning go reluctantly off, looking over his shoulder at me as if I'd find an excuse to save him from going. I never did, and I didn't think Sallie should have given him an easier job. To me, the point was to toughen him up, not protect him.

Ben Boy refused to leave the shoeshine business, however. "How would I know what's going on if I wasn't on the streets?" he asked belligerently. "No, I won't do it!"

We were in the shack and Sallie wasn't there to see his indignation, which I thought was a good thing.

"You don't have to," I said calmly. "I just wanted you to know she offered."

"Well," he said, mollified, "I'll thank her."

And thank her he did, with his best manners. After that, he came by the store even more frequently, so that I thought he might as well be working there. From time to time, I nudged him to get out the door and get about business. But he and Sallie became fast friends, trading news of the city they'd picked up from their respective customers. And sometimes they talked about Stephen McNutt's murder. Almost a month had gone by without any more action than Longhair Jim's gloom-filled visits, full of intrigue and threats from all directions, and an occasional message from Lambreth about his inability to settle the so-called estate.

"We ought to just forget about Longhair Jim and that fat lawyer and find that Judd Ambrose ourselves," Ben Boy said time and again.

And late one cold night in early March, at Ben Boy's urging, we started out to do just that. Ben Boy, Dickey-bird, July, and I all huddled on the pallets, cold enough to want to be close together but not yet sleepy enough to lie down.

"Sallie never will find out who killed her cousin," Ben Boy said disgustedly. "Longhair Jim keeps hinting at deep dark secrets like he was a gambler and maybe killed for that, and that lawyer fellow tells Sallie there's no money and the house is falling down. But we know the house ain't falling down."

Thinking aloud led Ben Boy into a long discussion of the perplexities of criminal investigation in general and Sallie's case in particular until Dickey-bird knocked us all over with a flat statement:

"We'll have to help her solve it. Not find Judd Ambrose, but find out who really killed him. Those other people—they're just trying to cheat her."

"Okay, wise guy," Ben Boy said, "just what are we supposed to do?"

"I don't know," he said, miserable now that he couldn't follow through with his brilliant idea. There was silence, each of us thinking of how we should go about helping her.

"We could go tell that lawyer we know he's trying to cheat her," Dickey-bird suggested.

"No," I said, "he wouldn't pay any attention to brats from the Acre. And we don't have any proof. It's just a hunch."

"Right," Ben Boy said. "We need evidence."

"Evidence . . . where can we find evidence?" I wondered.

"Let's start with the house," Ben Boy said. "We can sneak

inside and see what we find." In his enthusiasm, he jumped up and began to walk around the shack. "We'll go tonight . . ."

"Tonight?" I asked, somewhat alarmed. "I don't want to go anywhere tonight. It's cold out."

"Can't go in the daytime," Ben Boy said. "Somebody'd see us. July and Dickey-bird can stay here, and you and I will go. Won't take more'n an hour."

And that's how I found myself clutching my thin coat about me and trudging down Rusk Street with Ben Boy at near mid-night on a clear, cold evening. The moon was bright enough to light our way, and we ducked and dodged whenever we saw people coming who might question us about why we were out late at night. When there was no one in sight, we ran to keep ourselves warm. Breathless, we stopped at the gate to Stephen McNutt's house.

"Wow!" Ben Boy breathed. "That's a swell house."

"Don't stand there admiring," I said. "Let's get inside."

Ben Boy had many talents, among them a good strong ability to pick a lock. He worked quietly on the kitchen door for a few seconds, and we were inside.

"Check the kitchen drawers for papers or something," he said.

"I want to start in the parlor with the rugs and furniture that Sallie thought were so special," I said, barging past him.

As we crept along the bare hall floor, even our whispers seemed to echo. "Spooky, isn't it?" Ben Boy said. "The echo is weird."

"It echoes because it's empty," I said in normal loud tones as I turned through the sliding doors of the parlor. My voice scared Ben Boy so bad he slapped me hard on the head, and I would have hit him back but I was too confused by what I saw in front of me.

There was not a stick of furniture in the whole room—rugs, tables, chairs, lamps, the sofa Sallie admired, even bric-a-brac and pictures, were gone. All that hinted of the former luxury of the room was mahogany wainscoting and the brocaded walls.

"Wow!" That seemed to be Ben Boy's phrase for the evening. "You didn't say it was empty."

"It wasn't before."

Silently, we explored the rest of the huge house, upstairs and down, our way lit by moonlight streaming in the windows. There was some furniture in other rooms, but there was evidence of lots of missing pieces—an oriental rug remained in one bedroom but dents in it indicated where a desk had stood, a desk chair stood forlornly in the library with no desk in front of it though the library bookshelves were lined with leather-bound volumes, faded places on the wall indicated where pictures had hung. It was as though someone had come through and carefully picked what he wanted to take. Ben Boy opened drawers and prowled through papers in a chest of drawers, lighting a match to see, but found nothing that either one of us thought was important.

"Ben Boy, it's time to go home," I yawned, unable to see that we were doing anything to solve the murder.

In one swift motion, he blew out the match, grabbed my arm, and whispered, "Shhh!"

"What . . ."

But I said no more, for Ben Boy clamped a hand over my mouth. "Shhh!" he commanded again. "Listen!"

And then I heard voices, followed by footsteps on the verandah. The two men who approached seemed not the least bit concerned about the noise they made. Of course they're not, I thought—they don't expect us to be here.

I grabbed Ben Boy, pointing to the bedroom closet, and we crept into the safety of the darkness. Shivering, only partly from the cold, I clung to Ben Boy while we listened to the men walk about downstairs and mount the stairs. By then, we could hear their conversation.

"Somebody's been here," a voice said. "Kitchen door's open."

"Who'd be here?" asked another deep voice.

"That Miz McNutt, that's who," said the first one. "She best not be nosin' around down here."

Holding my breath, I grabbed Ben Boy. He squeezed back, as though to give us both courage. I wondered if I could stop a sneeze if it came.

The second voice chuckled. "It's her house, ain't it?"

"Not yet. Lambreth'll stall that for a long time. Least till we get all the good stuff outa here."

"Lady's liable to get impatient," the other voice said. "But she's not the kind to come prowlin' in an empty house. She'd go to Lambreth first and cause a fuss."

"She better." The voice had hard steel in its tone. "She best not mess this up. I find her nosin' around here, she won't nose around anything again. And that goes for them Acre brats that hang around her, too."

I was going to sneeze. I knew it. Pinching my nose shut, I held my breath until the feeling subsided.

"Come on," said the other, "let's get that vase and get going. Lambreth said it's on a dresser in the bedroom."

We could hear a match being struck to light the gas lamp and then, beneath the closet door, we saw the slight glow of the lamp.

"There!" said the deepest of the two voices. "Now who would think a little thing like that is worth $500?"

"Not me," was the answer. "But Lambreth knows somebody who'll pay that. Let's go."

Ben Boy had to hold tight to me so I wouldn't come leaping out of the closet in my anger. But the rush of anger passed, and I stayed quiet until long after we'd heard them slam the front door and clomp off the verandah.

Quietly we snuck to the front windows of the bedroom and peered out, only to be rewarded with the sight of two horsemen headed back up Samuels Avenue.

"Wow!" Ben Boy said. "Wonder what that vase looked like?" Ben Boy looked around, hoping perhaps to see another vase.

"I don't care," I said, more scared than I wanted to admit. "I just want to go home."

"Come on, Lizzie. Don't act like a girl now!"

"Ben Boy, I ain't actin' like a girl. I just . . . well, those men scared me."

"Well," he said, leading the way downstairs, "at least we know what's going on."

"What?" I asked, not sure I understood the whole thing.

"Lambreth's selling the furniture and stuff out of the house. But we can't tell Sallie about this."

"You're right," I said. "She'd come right down here . . . and you heard what that man said he'd do."

"He meant it," Ben Boy said.

Finally, dreading the long walk, we headed home, both more discouraged than heartened by what we'd found. We knew more than we did before, but it didn't seem it would do us much good.

"Why hasn't Longhair Jim discovered this if he's detecting this case?" Ben Boy wondered aloud, as we walked up Samuels Avenue.

"I don't think he's gone farther than the White Elephant," I scoffed.

"Lizzie," Ben Boy said solemnly, "we can't even tell Sallie we were down here tonight."

"All right," I said, too tired and cold to argue.

"Swear an oath," he insisted.

"Oh, for pity's sake," I said. "All right, I swear by my honor that I won't tell anyone."

We shook on it, and by that time we were back at the shack.

We slept until nearly noon the next day and then had to rush to the store, where an impatient Sallie paced back and forth.

"I thought you understood about people worrying about you," she said, obviously angry with me.

"We overslept," I said, "and I'm sorry. I really am."

"Overslept? Until noon? What time did you go to sleep?"

"It was late," I answered dumbly.

"What kept you up late?" she demanded.

If this was what having parents was like, I wanted no more of it. Here we'd been doing something for her, and I was getting scolded like a naughty child. And I couldn't even tell her what I'd been doing. If I could have, it would only have made her more angry that we were out on the streets at night.

"Oh, nothing," I said, "just fooling around." I never did learn to lie very convincingly.

Sallie gave me a long, hard look and turned to her desk.

But then something happened that took all our minds away from detecting and Stephen McNutt but sure did bring Longhair Jim's name to every tongue in town. Afterward everyone called it the Battle of Buttermilk Junction.

Ben Boy came shouting into the shack one night. "Lizzie, Lizzie . . ."

"Don't scare a person to death," I shouted back. "What in heaven's name's the matter?"

"It's a strike," he said breathlessly.

I was as cross as he was breathless, having thought perhaps the Acre was on fire or something. "What are you talking about?"

"The railroad. Half the city's down to the railroad yards, and the trains can't go anyplace."

We had heard vaguely that the Knights of Labor were striking, trying to free the railroads from Jay Gould. Down to Alvarado and up north by Dennison and Palestine, local railroad employees had struck, but those places were all far away, twenty-five miles or more, and we didn't pay much attention. No one thought it would come to our own backyard. Now it had. But in our lives, excitement was excitement, no matter what kind.

"There's a bunch of women, with their little kids, blocking the track down to the yards," Ben Boy said, "and half the city's gathered to watch. They been running engines at 'em to scare 'em away, but those women won't budge."

Ben Boy was right. Most of Fort Worth, at least the men of the city, was in the railroad yards, and each man carried a rifle or a shotgun. They milled around one particular train that wasn't going anywhere 'cause it had been uncoupled, and I saw two

men taking nuts and bolts out of the parts of the cars that
hooked together. They were sweaty, dirty men in work clothes,
but on the platform of one car, watching in disgust, were several
men in business suits, railroad officials I guessed. There was lots
of shouting, men waving their rifles, and yelling, but it didn't
look like there would be a riot.

Ben Boy found a spot on top of a small building, and by
hoisting and pushing we got July up there. Then Dickey-bird
and I followed, and the four of us sat down to wait, with front
row seats just in case anything exciting should happen.

"What's a strike?" Dickey-bird asked, his eyes wide with curiosity.

"Well," Ben Boy said loftily, "it's when the men, well, they get
together like this . . . and everybody's got to have a rifle . . .
and well, they . . ."

"It has something to do with not working," I said. "Sallie tried
to explain it to me the other day. The Knights of Labor say the
railroads ain't payin' them enough, and they block the trains to
force the railroads to give them more money."

"Wow!" was all Dickey could answer.

It was early March and still cool, and as the evening wore on,
we got colder and colder. July began to fuss until I threatened
her good that I'd hide her doll when we got home. The milling,
shouting, angry men below us frightened her, and she clutched
tight to my arm until I had a backache from her pulling on me.

We sat on the rooftop until nine or ten o'clock, and the big-
gest excitement we saw was one small fistfight, and at that it was
between two of the strikers. The railroad men stayed in their car
looking out the window at the strikers and all the spectators. It
was a disappointing adventure.

"Might as well go home," Ben Boy said. He had occasionally
climbed down from our roof to wander through the crowd and
see what he could learn. "Nothin's gonna happen tonight. And
they've sent for Rangers."

"Rangers?" Dickey-bird asked.

"Texas Rangers," Ben Boy said loftily, glad to show off his

knowledge. "They're the fastest draw, toughest, meanest men in the whole state."

"Wow!" That was Dickey-bird's favorite phrase. "Are they outlaws?"

" 'Course not. They're officers, kind of like deputy sheriffs, but they work for the whole state."

"Wow!"

Just as we climbed down from the roof to head home to a supper of cold cornbread, Ben Boy grabbed my arm and whispered, "Look."

There, striding through the crowd which parted to make room for him, was Longhair Jim. He stood out among the strikers because of his hair and that black, rumpled suit he always wore. And he carried no rifle. He ignored the catcalls and comments from the crowd, looking straight ahead, and went up the stairs and into the railroad car that held the train officials. Behind him, the crowd booed and called his name. They may have booed, but I thought he looked like I wanted Longhair Jim to look— self-confident, fearless, scornful of those who disagreed with him. Maybe, I thought hopefully, he's fixin' to be a hero again. In spite of Sallie, I would have liked to have him restored to that status.

"Wonder what he's doin?" I said aloud.

"Suppose he works for the railroad people?" Ben Boy suggested. "Won't make him popular in Fort Worth."

That was just what Longhair Jim did, though—he hired on with the railroad in command of their armed guard. The railroads were fed up with their trains not going nowhere, and they decided to move them no matter what.

Six

SALLIE PACED THE FLOOR, her chin in her hand just like we saw her the first day she arrived in the Acre. July and I waited, wondering which way her thoughts would go.

"Lizzie, I don't want you to go back to the railroad yards."

"But what if there's more goin' on? Ben Boy's down there now."

"I do not want any of you to go, because I think it's dangerous."

Sallie presented me with a real problem. I'd never in my life been told what to do, and I wasn't about to let that start now. In one way, she was forcing me to go back to the yards, just to show that I could take care of myself.

But at the same time, I was beginning to understand, because of Sallie even more than July, about the ties that bind people together. I owed Sallie not because she was good to me but because I admired her and liked her. Somehow that gave me an obligation. July had taught me about dependence. Sallie was teaching me the limits of independence. I was utterly confused.

"Lizzie?"

"Yes, ma'am." If she asked me to promise, if she forced the issue, I would have to refuse. I waited for her to go on.

"Just remember that I care about you—and Ben Boy and July and Dickey—and I don't want you hurt. It's not that I don't think it's proper, though a body could make a good argument in that direction too. You think about it."

She had put the responsibility on me. Oh, I could sneak to the yards and she'd never know, but I would know. Sallie had just ruined one of the most exciting things to happen in the Acre in a long while.

I stayed away from the strike, though it cost me dearly. But I also stayed away from the store. To have gone there would have been like reporting in, like saying, "See? I'm being good," and I couldn't do that. I sent Dickey-bird to help Sallie every morning, but July and I stayed at the shack, running errands for Lulabelle and doing all the things I used to do before Sallie came to Fort Worth. It was boring, and I itched to be in the store. Every night for three days when Ben Boy and Dickey-bird came in, I questioned them tirelessly for details of the day.

Ben Boy, not having the obligation I did, went back to the yards. "All hell's gonna' break loose tomorrow," he said one night. "The railroads are gonna run the blockade, with Longhair Jim in charge. They've thrown the switches all through town so they can't get derailed, and they're putting armed guards at every window."

Sallie will never know, I thought. I'll swear July to secrecy, and we'll go watch the fun. With that thought in mind, I went to sleep anticipating an exciting day. I'd see Longhair Jim in action, maybe even some shooting. But come morning, I found I couldn't do it.

"Ain't you goin'?" Ben Boy asked incredulously.

"Naw," I said listlessly. "You tell me about it. And Ben Boy, you be careful and take a care of Dickey-bird. It's dangerous with all those guns flashing in the air." I sounded like Sallie, I thought.

I found out soon enough that I wouldn't have seen the excitement anyway. Nothing happened until the train was miles off down the track, at a place called Buttermilk Junction. The railroad folks hadn't thought far enough ahead to fix the switches out in the country, and as the train came along, two men stepped out from hiding and pulled the switch. The train stopped, and the guards climbed out, and there was a real gun battle, just as I thought. Only Ben Boy didn't see it either; he was still back at the yards in Fort Worth. But he heard about it there, soon as word came in.

"Longhair Jim saw these men walking away from the railroad tracks, and I guess he thought they were going to blow up the track or something, because he ordered them to stop. By the time he saw the men with rifles hidden in the grass, Jim and the railroad officials were out in the open, with no rifles and no cover. The strikers blasted away—pow, pow, pow—" Ben Boy interrupted his narration to imitate rifle shots. "A deputy sheriff was killed and two other men were hit. They didn't have time to shoot back, and they couldn't see no one to shoot anyway. Those men were hiding everywhere, in bushes and grass along the track." Ben Boy was breathless as he related this excitement.

"What happened to Jim?" I asked.

"He got two bullet holes in his hat."

And more in his reputation, I thought. Longhair Jim had made a serious mistake. "Did they just stop fighting?"

"I guess so. Maybe they saw they'd actually killed a man, and that made 'em stop," Ben Boy said. "That deputy that died wasn't but nineteen years old, they said, and had a wife and a little baby. Railroad folks are takin' up a big collection for him."

"I bet his wife'd rather have him than the money," I said.

Even though he wasn't hit, something bad happened to Long-hair Jim in the battle at Buttermilk Junction. I was right about his reputation. He lost it, along with his connections. He'd tried to play a double hand, working for the railroad and still claimin' to be a friend of the people, and you could say folks resented it mightily. Fact is, some militiamen came up from downstate to restore order, but they came as much as anything to protect Longhair Jim.

By that time I didn't have to go to the yards for excitement. It was all around me in town. Somebody started the rumor that the strikers were going to break into the stores to steal guns, and then were going to burn the depot. Lots of men in town turned out with their rifles to patrol, and you could tell they were all nervous as cats, waiting to hear those three taps on the fire bell that meant trouble.

Sallie slept at the store a couple of nights and kept the lamps burning bright. I knew that because Ben Boy and Dickey-bird stayed with her, which caused me untold grief. I longed to be there, too, but my stubborn pride got in the way.

Sallie would not hear of loading one of the rifles that she had for sale. The only protection they had was themselves. I thought they were poorly protected, though I knew Sallie could talk down just about anybody. Dickey-bird said it was spooky, being inside and hearing all that shouting on the streets, late at night. To me, it sounded like an adventure, and I longed for Sallie to apologize so that I could go back.

The excitement came and went, and the strike was settled, with no permanent damage, except the one man who was killed, and Longhair Jim who'd lost face in Fort Worth. Ben Boy began to come home with stories of Longhair Jim drunk in this bar, or boasting about his marksmanship in that one. He was a man desperate to salvage his reputation, and he decided one way to do it was to solve Stephen McNutt's murder once and for all.

I had been away from the store near a week without word from Sallie when I finally gave in. "Come on, July," I said one morning. "We're going to see Sallie."

July clapped her hands and packed up her dolls, and we headed for McNutt's Mercantile, me planning all the while what I would say. I reached the door of the store without a word in my head and walked silently in.

Sallie was waiting on a customer, and she barely nodded at me. When she was free, she looked in my direction and said, all business, "I think the storeroom needs straightening, if you don't mind, Lizzie."

Relieved, I went to work on the storeroom, which really

wasn't all that bad. But I tidied up shelves and swept the floor
and dusted the canned goods.

After a bit, Sallie came and stood in the door. "I've missed
you," she said simply.

"I was busy," I said.

"Yes, I understand. Dickey told me that you were running
errands for Mrs. Browning and the like . . ."

"Lulabelle needed me," I interrupted angrily, but I was only
angry because I was embarrassed.

". . . and that you did not go back to the railroad yards."

"Yeah, I didn't. Didn't want to," I said, sweeping furiously and
staring at the floor as though I could will the dust away.

"Lizzie, look at me. Did you stay away because I asked you
to?"

"Well, that too," I said reluctantly.

"I appreciate that," she said. "And I'm glad you've come back.
I truly did miss you." With that, she walked back into the main
part of the store and never ever said another word about the
whole thing, never said I was being foolish or spiteful or child-
ish. And she never tried to hug me, as lots of women would
have, for I guess she knew that would have spooked me. Sallie
just let it go. I learned a big lesson that day.

The first thing Longhair Jim did was go to Mr. Lambreth. Why
he hadn't done that weeks before, I never could puzzle out. But
if they were both working to solve the murder, seems to me
they would have gotten together. Course I knew Lambreth
wasn't working that way at all. But far as I knew, Longhair Jim
didn't know the truth about the fat lawyer. Sometimes, thinking
about it all got so complicated that it made my head spin, and I
was grateful to sweep out the storeroom or do something else
simple.

Longhair Jim came walking into the store one afternoon, not
weaving this time but still smelling strongly of whisky. His eyes
had a haunted look, like a man who's had his moment of glory
and doesn't know what to do with the rest of his life.

"I think I'm on to something," he announced with a grand sweep of his arm. "Been a little slow about it, 'cause I had another problem to take care of. But now we got those railroads runnin' again, I can turn my attention to my other cases, like your problem, Miz McNutt." He stood, chest puffed out, waiting for Sallie to say something about his bravery and courage at Buttermilk Junction, but all she said was "Oh?"

Dickey-bird and I snuck up close to Sallie's desk, so's we could hear what the big new discovery was, but July crept off to a far corner of the store where she busied herself with her doll. We weren't sneaky enough, because Longhair Jim saw us.

"Damn Acre brats!" he exploded. "Can't for the life of me figure why you let them hang around here, ma'am."

"They are my employees and my friends," Sallie said calmly. "Now, Mr. Courtright, your news?"

"Oh, yeah, my news." He pulled a chair around to face Sallie and sprawled into it. "You don't happen to have anything to drink around here, do you? That railroad strike got to my nerves somethin' awful."

"I can imagine," Sallie said in a kind of puzzling manner. "But no. We do not stock liquor."

"Just thought I'd ask. Well, I was over talkin' to ole Walter Lambreth this morning."

Sallie gasped, and then I thought she'd grin, but she managed to control herself. She must have thought what I did, that Longhair Jim and Walter Lambreth were a mismatched pair if ever there was one. I bet Mr. Lambreth could barely stand to have the famed gunman in his office.

"Ole Walter tells me he had to go once, on business mind you, to the White Elephant, and he saw McNutt at the faro table upstairs."

"Mr. Lambreth went there once?" Sallie questioned. "Mr. Courtright, I saw him the day I met you there, and Stephen was long dead by then."

"Well, now, ma'am, I didn't say only once, but that once when he saw McNutt, that was the important time."

"And what does it prove?"

Longhair Jim threw his hands up in the air as though completely exasperated. "Prove? Why, ma'am, it proves just what I've been tryin' to tell you. Stephen McNutt, your goody-goody cousin, was up to his ears in trouble with the gambling crowd in this town."

Sallie stiffened and spoke through clenched teeth. "That Mr. McNutt once played faro at the White Elephant is not proof he was 'up to his ears,' as you put it. And I have never claimed that my late husband's cousin"—she emphasized the relationship—"was a better man than anyone else. I never knew him, but I do resent your use of the term 'goody-goody.' "

Jim got up and began to pace. "Now, look here, Miz McNutt, let's face facts. You hired me to do a job, and I'm doin' the best I can. If I've insulted you, I'm sorry, but I've got to call a spade a spade." He gestured largely again, and then sank back into the chair.

"I understand, Mr. Courtright, but since there has never been any question of a fee exchanged, I cannot say that I hired you. Nonetheless, I do appreciate your efforts. Now if you'll excuse me, I have book work to do."

Longhair Jim was dismissed, and he knew it. But even then he tried to save face. "Got to be goin' myself. Got things to do, over to the White Elephant and around." With that, he doffed his hat, bowed low, and swaggered out the door.

"You know," Sallie said thoughtfully after he'd left, "Mrs. Browning was right. I think that man's trouble."

Part of the trouble he caused walked in the door not an hour later in the form of Mr. Walter Lambreth. Ben Boy had stopped by for one of his frequent visits by then, so we all got to listen to what the lawyer had to say. This time we hid ourselves better behind some counters, and Lambreth had no idea we were there. Sallie knew, though, and made a gesture behind her back calling for silence when we began to whisper.

Lambreth walked directly through the store, looking around

as he approached Sallie's desk. "Business a little slow?" he asked.

"Not at all," Sallie replied, remaining seated at her desk. "My gross receipts for the past week are almost as good as Stephen's. I've studied his ledgers."

Lambreth paused for just a minute, and I wondered if he wasn't damning himself for not taking up those ledgers so Sallie wouldn't see that the store ran at a profit. But then he was all jovial again. "Quite the little businesswoman, Miss McNutt. I must say you're doing better than I expected."

"Thank you," Sallie said, with just a touch of sarcasm edging her voice. "What can I do for you today, Mr. Lambreth?"

"I came to talk to you about Courtright, Miss McNutt. Frankly, he's an embarrassment, and I don't think it right for you to associate with him *or* with some of your other close acquaintances."

"Are you referring to the children, Mr. Lambreth?"

"Uh, yes . . . yes, I am." He rolled his hat in his hands and looked uncomfortable.

"The children have nothing to do with any business relationship I have with you. And I don't associate, as you put it, with Mr. Courtright."

"You hired him!" the lawyer burst out. "I call that associating."

"I did not hire him, and I will not pay him a fee. He simply wanted to work on the puzzle of Stephen's murder, for the good of the community."

"The good of the community? Dear heaven, madam, Longhair Jim Courtright never thought of any good but his own. It's incredible how naïve some of you easterners can be when you get out here."

"I doubt that geography has much to do with it," Sallie said coldly. "Now, Mr. Lambreth, I would like to review these account books with you at your convenience. They show that Stephen made a good profit every month for the past three years. Where is that money?"

"How am I to know? I was his lawyer, not his accountant. For all I know, he mailed it back to you or threw it away in a prairie breeze." Lambreth was obviously impatient and angry, his face turning red and his fists clenching and opening over and over again.

I motioned for Ben Boy to follow me, on the floor, behind the counters, to the far end of the store where we could whisper.

"I have an idea," I said softly. "I think you should follow Mr. Lambreth and see where he goes and what he does."

Ben Boy nodded. "Good idea. But for how long? I got shoes to shine, you know, and last I checked you weren't paying for detective work neither."

"Don't follow him all the time. Just kind of off and on, get an idea of what he usually does."

"Okay."

Lambreth was taking his leave by then, still angry and huffy. "Good day, Miss McNutt. I shall inform you of any developments," he said, stalking out.

"Good day," Sallie called after him.

Ben Boy and I stood up, and Ben Boy sauntered toward the door, clutching his bootblack box and looking casual. Without a word to us, he followed Lambreth out the door, at a distance, of course.

"Where's Ben Boy going?" Sallie asked.

"Oh, just out to find some dusty shoes," I replied vaguely. "Sallie, if Mr. Lambreth doesn't know where all that money went, who would?"

"I don't know, Lizzie, I really don't know." She shook her head. "But I don't think Mr. Courtright is the one to ask. I decided not to tell him about it."

I nodded. "I won't say anything to anybody," I swore, crossing my heart, which made Sallie laugh aloud, and I was glad to hear that deep laugh. But I worried about all the secrets I held. I couldn't tell Sallie about the missing furniture at McNutt's house, and I couldn't tell Jim about the ledgers at the store. What if I made a mistake and said the wrong thing to the wrong person?

Sallie went to work at the desk again, singing softly about Dublin's fair city, where girls are so pretty. I was polishing the wood in the display counters at the other side of the store, and as I worked I tried humming a bit of "Barb'ra Allen," which I knew by now from hearing it so often. But it didn't sound right.

I loved the smell of the store. A mixture of leather and wood and tobacco, it was a smell all its own, and some days I took a deep breath when I walked through the door and just stood there, sniffing.

On a cold, windy day in March, July and I arrived bundled up in new warm clothes. The material was from Sallie and the sewing was done by Mrs. Straight, since Sallie no longer had time to sew—a fact which Lulabelle regretted greatly.

"I wish she'd forget that store and just work for me," Lulabelle sighed one day, and I all but laughed, wishing I could tell the kindly madam how unlikely that was!

This particular day as July and I went into the store, I didn't stop to breathe deep and enjoy being in the store, because curiosity got the best of me. A tall cowboy, his well-used boots and battered hat telling clearly that he had just come off the prairie, had walked in just in front of me, and I heard him say, "Mornin', ma'am. Where's my friend McNutt?"

Sallie turned a little pale. It's hard to say to someone, "Your friend is dead." But that's what she said, and the cowboy stood there with his mouth open, staring at her, for a full minute. It gave me time to study him. He was neither young nor old, but somewhere in the middle, like Sallie. His face was tan and creased by his eyes and mouth, so that he looked like what he was—a man who worked outdoors winter and summer, day and night.

He held his hat in his hands and ran one hand through blondish curly hair. "Dead?" he repeated, as though sure he'd been mistaken.

Sallie, who was often a mite touchy with strangers, softened at his dismay. "Mr. McNutt, my late cousin, was murdered last December."

"Your cousin?" He didn't seem to be able to speak beyond turning her answers into questions.

"Actually my late husband's cousin," Sallie explained. "I never knew him except by correspondence. But I had come here to work in his store."

The man looked around the store slowly, his eyes finally resting on July and me. He favored us with a nod and a slight "Howdy," and turned again to Sallie. "He was one of the best men I ever knew," he said. "Gave me supplies on credit to make that first drive up the trail, near fifteen years ago. Wasn't nothin' but a button myself then, but I never did forget. Been doin' my stockin' up and visitin' with him every spring since."

Sallie smiled. "I've found Stephen had many loyal customers," she said. "He must have been a good man."

"Yes, ma'am, he was. But you said murdered. They know who did it?"

"A man who worked for him is the principal suspect, but he has disappeared."

"They've got to find him," the man said fiercely. "They've got to." Then he dug in his pocket and drew out a crumpled list. "Well, I best be gettin' these supplies together. Name's Peters, ma'am, Sandy Peters. Reckon you'll find a ledger page in my name if you care to look."

Sallie called me to come and help Mr. Peters find his supplies, while she looked up his previous orders. Something about Mr. Peters seemed friendly and real, and even July took to him, following both of us around the store as we went about collecting flour and sugar and coffee and beans and all the necessaries to run a cow camp.

"Might be my last trail drive," he said conversationally. "But might not. Tried them railroad cars last year, but Texas cattle got horns too long. They get in a terrible mess packed into a railroad car. Naw, I'm gonna' do it the tried and true way this year. But you can't hardly beat them railroads for saving time and money."

His talk filled me with curiosity about the trail, and I wished, for just a minute, that I was a boy so I could go with him. Just as quickly I thought I'd make sure Ben Boy didn't cross paths with this Sandy Peters or he'd leave his shoeshine box behind and head up the trail to see the elephant.

"You know McNutt?" he asked me conversationally.

"No, sir."

"Well, he was a fine man, a really fine man. I sure hope they catch the one what done it."

Now ordinarily I was pretty closemouthed, but Sandy Peters seemed so trustworthy, my tongue got loosened, even as I counted sacks of coffee. "Sallie's got help. Longhair Jim is trying to find out who did it, and Mr. McNutt's lawyer, Mr. Lambreth, is kind of advising her."

"Longhair Jim?" he asked in disgust. "Don't think he'll do much good lessen there's a reward in it."

"There's not," I said, the wheels going around in my mind. "At least not yet." A reward, I was thinking, might make somebody come forward who knew where Judd Ambrose was and at least his guilt or innocence would be solved, once and for all. "Then maybe somebody'd find that Ambrose fellow," I said aloud, giving voice to my thoughts.

"Ambrose? Not Judd Ambrose?"

"That's him," I said, figuring he'd known Ambrose sometime in the past.

"Judd Ambrose signed on out to the cow camp, oh, 'bout Christmastime, a little before. You sure about this, miss?"

"Sure I'm sure. Judd Ambrose worked for Mr. McNutt, but he got fired 'cause he was drunk, and then he disappeared right when Mr. McNutt was murdered, and everybody, well, at least most folks think he did it. Ask Sallie."

So there we were, all three blabbing at once about Judd Ambrose, standing in the middle of the store with a huge order of supplies stacked all around us, when Longhair Jim himself came swaggering in.

He did not look pleased to see Sandy Peters. "Peters," he acknowledged, nodding his head ever so slightly.

"Jim," came the answering nod.

"If you'll excuse me, I have business with the lady." Longhair Jim took Sallie's arm and tried to propel her to the back of the store, but Sallie gently pulled her arm back and stepped away from him.

"Mr. Peters was just telling us that Judd Ambrose works for him at his ranch."

The cowboy laughed. "Call me Sandy, please, ma'am. And my spread ain't hardly got enough buildings to call it a ranch. But, yeah, Ambrose is out there. Fine fellow. I can't believe he done it. I know he had a little problem with the bottle back here in town, but murder? Naw, not Ambrose."

Longhair Jim whirled toward him. "Exactly. I've been trying to convince this lovely lady that Judd Ambrose is not the killer."

"Well," Sandy said, "he told me when he rode up that he'd had a problem back here in Fort Worth that had got him fired. Course I had no idea it was my old friend McNutt what fired him."

"I've told Mrs. McNutt here Ambrose didn't do it," Longhair Jim repeated. "There's a lot more involved than a drunken, fired employee."

"Like what?" Sandy asked.

"Gamblin'. I think the White Elephant's mixed up in it, maybe more." He lowered his voice to a whisper, even though nobody but us was in the store.

Sandy did the unforgivable then. He laughed aloud, a great roaring laughter that filled the store and bounced off the tin ceiling, a laughter so infectious that soon Sallie was covering her mouth with a polite hand and I was grinning from ear to ear.

July looked up at me and solemnly asked, "What's funny?"

"Nothin's funny, you brat!" Longhair Jim roared and tried to make a swipe at her when she stuck her tongue out.

"Mr. Courtright!" Sallie said. "Please do not talk to the children that way." All laughter was gone now.

"I can see I'll get no business done here today," he said huffily and stormed out of the store.

"Ma'am?" Sandy asked. "How did you get mixed up with him? He's pure trouble waitin' to happen."

"You're not the first to say that," Sallie said with discouragement. "But since I never hired him, I can't fire him."

I itched to tell Sandy that Ben Boy and I were working on the case and all about the missing things at the house, but I was still bound by my oath to Ben Boy.

"Is the marshal looking for Ambrose?" Sandy asked.

"Officially, yes," Sallie said.

"Guess I best get on out to camp and bring him back then. But I'll warrant he's the wrong man. He's a good fellow."

Sandy loaded his supplies into a buckboard while Sallie totaled up his bill. He paid cash, joking about not needing the credit any more, and he was gone.

"Takes three days to get this buckboard out there," he said. "Might be 'most a week 'fore I get back."

A week seemed a long time to be uncertain and waiting, but then we'd been uncertain and waiting for months now. We could wait another week.

"Lizzie," Sallie said as we turned away from the door, "I'm not going to tell Walter Lambreth about this. I don't know why, but some instinct says not to."

I thought it was a good instinct, but I couldn't tell Sallie that.

Seven

JULY TOOK SICK that week when Sandy Peters was off to bring Judd Ambrose back, and I spent all my time nursing her. Poor thing had a high fever and seemed to choke a lot when she wanted to catch her breath.

"Croup," Sophronia told me solemnly. "Ain't nothin' you can do for it. Takes 'em quick about this age."

" 'Phronie," I shouted, "get out of here sounding like doom itself. She's just got a cold. She'll be fine."

But I worried. I knew just enough to know that Sophronia was right. I'd seen a little boy die of croup two years before, with his mama, who lived and worked in one of the cribs, holding his head and begging him to breathe. She couldn't afford a doctor, and none had come to help her, though it might not have done any good anyway. Lulabelle told me that croup just closes up a baby's throat, "swells it shut," she said, and the child can't breathe.

July coughed in great, deep hacking sounds, and she was listless, like a limp puppy lying there on her pallet. Lulabelle had sent 'Phronie over with hot broth. She wouldn't come herself, of course, feeling the way she did about catching kinds of sickness. But July just stuck her tongue in the spoonful I held up for her and then fell back on the pallet.

Ben Boy brought her a candy stick, filched I'm sure from the sweet shop, but even that didn't tempt her, though she did smile at him and murmur, "Ben Boy good."

Of course I didn't get to the store. Dickey-bird carried word back and forth between me and Sallie, who was mightily worried about July, according to my messenger. But I told her we were doing all we knew to do for July, and she was bound to be better soon. Only it was a lie, and I knew it.

July got worse and worse, lying there with her face gleaming wet and her tiny body shivering and torn by that deep coughing.

The third day that I stayed with July, Sallie closed the store and came to the Acre. Dickey-bird trailed behind her.

"You what?" I demanded, as angry at her as I'd ever been, and feeling beholden when I didn't want to feel that way. Folks just didn't close their stores in the middle of the day, though I full well understood she couldn't have left Dickey-bird in charge.

"I closed the store so I could come see about July. I did not particularly want to come to this, uh, neighborhood at night."

"Smart." I grinned in spite of myself. "July'll be fine." I said it with a bravado I didn't feel.

Sallie was on her knees by July's bed. "Not unless we do something for her, she won't," Sallie said. "She's got the croup. Funny thing to have in spring, though."

"What does the time of year matter?"

"Sometimes you can take croupy children out in the cold air, and they can breathe better. But steam is the other thing that works." She stood up and took a few steps away from July's pallet, so we could talk.

"Steam?" How, I wondered, did she know all this and all Lulabelle and 'Phronie could do was shake their stupid heads. Would steam have saved that other little boy?

"A boiling kettle or pan of water," she said patiently.

"We ain't got anything to boil it on," Dickey-bird said, putting the obvious into words.

"We'll take her to Nellie's," Sallie announced, without so much as a by-your-leave. "It's shameful enough that children like you have to live in these conditions, but when there's illness . . ."

Her sentence trailed off, but there was no mistaking the anger in her voice. "Why hasn't Mrs. Browning done something?"

"She did," I said. "She sent 'Phronie with broth, only July won't touch it."

"Broth," Sallie said in disgust. "This child needs warmth and a comfortable bed and a steam kettle—in a real house, not this godforsaken shack."

I started to defend my home, but decided it was useless. Sallie went right on talking anyway. "We'll get her to Nellie. She'll give her proper care."

"Wait a minute," I interrupted. "We can't just take her to Mrs. Straight without asking, and we sure can't all end up landing at her house. I can watch her better here." I folded my arms in front of me as though that ended the subject.

Sallie's question was blunt. "Watch her die?" she asked.

Dickey-bird's face turned white, and I gulped. We would take her to Mrs. Straight's, of course, but how?

"How're you gonna get her there?" I asked. Frightened, I had made the whole thing Sallie's responsibility. Somehow when July was in the shack, even if she wasn't getting better, I was in control. If we took her to Mrs. Straight's, I'd lost a little piece of my world. Logic told me I wouldn't let July die to save my pride, but I still balked some.

"Mrs. Browning has a carriage. I've seen her in it, though I have no idea who drives it for her."

"Whoever's handy," I said, knowing more about Lulabelle than Sallie could ever learn as an outsider. "And she's not likely to let July in it if she's got something catching."

"Catching? Oh, for heaven's sake," Sallie exploded. "This child's life is at stake."

Sallie forgot herself and spoke too loud, and July, who had been lying quietly on her pallet watching us with wide eyes, burst into great loud sobs. Between sobs, she cried out, "Don't wanna die! Don't wanna die!"

I threw Sallie an "I told you so" look, though it beat me why I

should have my nose out of joint that she was doing exactly what I wanted—taking responsibility for July at a time when I had no idea what to do.

Kneeling to reassure July, Sallie spoke over her shoulder to Dickey-bird. "Go to Mr. Courtright. I imagine you'll find him at the White Elephant. Tell him it's important that he hurry. And Dickey, after he's on his way, go on to Mrs. Straight's and tell her to get things ready for July."

It wasn't just the way I felt—I had been pushed aside. I stood there, useless, while Dickey-bird set off on important errands, and Sallie crooned softly to July. She sang about Scarborough Fair and parsley, sage, rosemary, and thyme, her voice so soothing that even I sat down on the floor and listened quietly.

Finally, July slept, and Sallie and I sat by her without speaking for what seemed the longest time.

"I don't think he'll come," I whispered, breaking the silence but trying not to wake July. "He won't do anything for July. He hates all of us Acre brats, but her most particular."

Sallie grinned. "It's because she sticks her tongue out at him. No, he wouldn't come for July. But he'll come for me," she said confidently.

I wished I felt as sure.

After a few minutes, Sallie spoke. "I've a mind to report this to . . . oh, I don't know who. Maybe Mr. Paddock that runs the newspaper."

"Report what?"

"That there are children living untended in conditions like this. Seems to me any respectable person would be outraged."

"Ain't nobody you could report it to who doesn't already know," I said practically. I was alarmed that she would consider drawing public attention to us like that. Sallie had a lot to learn about the way of the world.

"I can't believe that," Sallie replied and sank into a silence that did little to hide how rapidly her mind was working.

About two hours after we'd sent Dickey-bird, we heard the

clip-clop of horses' hooves and the squeak of wheels coming to a stop out in front of Lulabelle's.

"Run tell him to come around here," Sallie said, "but don't let him come in. He'd scare her. I'll carry July outside to the carriage."

I wanted to protest that July was too heavy, but I was afraid to argue with Sallie, and I did as I was told. The carriage she expected turned out to be a small, closed-in hack, with none other but Longhair Jim himself on the driver's seat. He merely looked at me in disgust when I told him Sallie wanted him in back at the shack, but he was all smiles and charm by the time he got back there. My hero sure had two faces—and I didn't much like either one of them.

"Ma'am, I had to borrow this rig. My apologies for taking so long."

Sallie smiled at him sweetly over July's head, which was buried in covers on her shoulder. "It's so kind of you to help me," she said. "Would you take us to Nellie's? This poor child is burning up and very sick." I was sure Sallie was being nicer than usual to him because she needed his help.

"Delighted to be of service," he said, holding her elbow to help her up into the hack while Sallie still clutched her burden. Roughly, he motioned for me to follow her, though I'd been hoping to sit on the driver's seat.

Longhair Jim pushed that horse, and we fairly flew through the streets. I think he was showing off his skills with the reins for Sallie, but her attention was so fixed on July she never seemed to notice. I was a little alarmed at our recklessness, not having ridden in coaches much anyway if at all, but we reached Mrs. Straight's safely and in record time.

Sallie barely thanked him at the gate, running into the house with July, and it was left to me to dismiss Longhair Jim.

"I'll just wait a bit," he said, hitching the horse to a piece of fence. "Miz McNutt might need further assistance." He smoothed the vest of his rumpled black suit in a preening gesture.

"Suit yourself," I said and left him standing there. Wasn't my house to invite him into anyway. Inside all was a bustle of activity. Mrs. Straight had two tea kettles boiling and a pallet made for July in the kitchen. She had draped chairs with blankets tent-fashion over the pallet, and she and Sallie would take turns holding first one and then the other kettle under the tent so July breathed in that steam. Mrs. Straight gave me one kettle and motioned for me to shuttle it back and forth from stove to tent, while she stirred a chicken she had put on to boil and ladled out a bowl of the broth to feed July. Dickey-bird, having beaten us to Mrs. Straight's house, sat quietly in a corner, watching with wide eyes.

Within an hour's time, July's coughing had stopped, and she had taken five spoonfuls of broth before drifting off into a sleep so peaceful that it alarmed me.

"Is she . . . is she . . . ?" I didn't really think she had totally stopped breathing, but she sure was quiet.

"She's better," Sallie said, wiping a loose strand of hair out of her eyes. "We can go back to the store."

The store! I'd forgotten all about it and how mad I was at Sallie for closing it, and all about Stephen McNutt and Sandy Peters and Judd Ambrose, and even all about Longhair Jim.

"Longhair Jim!" I exclaimed. "Bet he's still waiting outside." I ran through the dining room, past the long table, and through the parlor with its stiff, horsehair furniture. Pulling aside one of Mrs. Straight's lace curtains, I peeked out. Sure enough, there he stood, patiently leaning against the hack.

"Sallie!" I called so loud it's a wonder he didn't hear me. "He's still there."

"Oh, dear heaven," she said, coming through the house. "Well, there's nothing for it but to invite him in." Opening the door, with its oval cut-glass panel, she called out, "Mr. Courtright, won't you come in? I'm so sorry to have left you standing there."

"No matter," he said gallantly. "The child's welfare was the first concern."

Sallie made a motion behind her back when she heard me
snicker at his concern. "You're very kind," she said as he came
onto the porch. "The child is much better, thank you. Were it not
for your success in borrowing a hack, we could not have gotten
her here. Won't you join us for a cup of coffee?"

Awkwardly, Longhair Jim settled himself on the horsehair
sofa, sitting stiffly, which was what that sofa made you do. Nellie came in bearing a tray of coffee and homemade bread.

"Good day, Jim," she said. "We're beholden."

"Ma'am" was all he said, standing up like a perfect gentleman,
but I sensed that they knew each other and, like a lot of people,
Mrs. Straight didn't particularly care for Longhair Jim Courtright.
He, on the other hand, seemed slightly afraid of her or maybe of
what she could say.

Conversation over coffee would have been dull if it weren't
for Longhair Jim, who wanted to talk about the murder. "Waste
of time sending Peters back out for Ambrose, pure waste of
time. Ambrose didn't do it. There's a couple of faro ladies at the
White Elephant I intend to question more thoroughly."

"Faro ladies?" Sallie echoed. "You think Stephen was mixed
up in gambling or with the ladies or what?"

"Maybe a little of both," he said knowingly.

Sallie's chin went up and her expression stiffened. "Mr. Courtright, I've told you, I don't intend to have Stephen's reputation
suffer."

"But, Miz Sallie"—she hated it when he called her Miss Sallie
—"you wouldn't want to hide the truth now."

Changing the subject, she asked, "Does the marshal have an
arrest warrant out for Mr. Ambrose?"

"Well, now, yes ma'am, he does. But I can get it canceled,
since we know Mr. Ambrose didn't commit the murder."

"I don't believe Mr. Peters would want you to pull strings to
get the warrant erased," Sallie said primly. "It's best to let Mr.
Ambrose come forward and clear his name."

Longhair Jim looked disgusted, and after a few more comments about his theory on the murder, he took his leave, amid lots of thanks from Sallie and Mrs. Straight and silence from me and Dickey-bird.

We never did go back to the store that day. It was mid-afternoon by the time Longhair Jim left, and Sallie said she, for one, was whipped, "just whipped." I gathered she meant she was tired.

"Now," she said firmly, "you and Dickey-bird go get enough things to last you a few days, and find Ben Boy and tell him to do the same. You can all stay here, can't they, Nellie?"

Mrs. Straight looked alarmed. "I . . . well, I don't mean to be inhospitable, Sallie, but I got a new boarder comin' tomorrow, and, well . . . there plain isn't room."

"But that . . . that shack is where July got so sick."

"Well, now, I surely don't mean for them to take that little one back there. I'm gonna nurse her until she's well." Plainly, Nellie Straight thought that was the extent of her duty as a good Christian woman.

I was flat relieved. "Sallie, we belong in the Acre. That's where we live. If Mrs. Straight can take care of July until she's better, I'll be most grateful." It was a long and carefully thought-out speech for me, and I kind of sighed at the end. It would have made me nervous as an old hen to stay at Mrs. Straight's, much as I longed for a real bed with flowers on the coverlet.

"Me too," Dickey-bird whispered.

Sallie glared at me as though I had spoken out of turn, but she said nothing.

"We got to be goin'," I said. "Ben Boy will find the store closed and us not at the shack and he won't know what's happenin'."

Sallie was thinking again and had barely heard me speak. "Oh," she answered vaguely, "I'll see you both tomorrow morning."

"Yes, ma'am. And Sallie, Mrs. Straight, we sure do thank you. I guess July would be a goner if you hadn't helped us."

Sallie came alert. "Yes, she would have," she said fiercely.

Ben Boy laughed at us when we got back to the shack. "You had a chance to stay in a real house, and you turned it down? Dumb, dumb, dumb!"

I couldn't have made him understand, because I really didn't understand it myself. But we didn't belong at Mrs. Straight's, and I'd get July back as soon as she was well.

"Lizzie, Dickey," Sallie greeted us first thing the next morning, "we're going to do things a little differently from now on."

"Yes, ma'am?" I said cautiously.

"I'm going to wait on customers. You two will have certain chores, like dusting and sweeping and straightening merchandise. But you will also have lessons."

"Lessons!" Dickey-bird howled.

"Lessons," Sallie said firmly.

Before we knew it, we were seated at a table she cleared in the back of the store, and each of us had a tablet and pencil.

"Write your names and then the entire alphabet," Sallie commanded. "I'm going to get some readers, but for the time being, we'll have to start without. Can you each write the alphabet?"

We nodded and set to it, though with much chewing of the tongues and heavy use of the erasers on our pencils. My brief time at school had been long ago and never taken too seriously anyway.

And so the morning went. Sallie dictated words for us to spell —cat, dog, book, bell, and so on—and when a customer came in, she left us to wait on him. We were supposed to jump up and do our chores while she was busy, but the minute the customer left, she became a teacher again, and we were to hop back to that table. The getting up and down made me more tired than anything else, and I was surely glad when noon came.

"That's enough for today," Sallie decreed. "I don't want to overburden you."

"No, ma'am," I muttered, making Sallie laugh aloud.

"I'll get myself a real switch if there's any backtalk from my pupils," she threatened. "Now, Nellie expects you two for dinner so that you can see July, and you'll bring me back a sack."

July was sitting on the kitchen floor, bundled in a great big sweater of Mrs. Straight's and playing with a doll we'd brought with her the day before. When she saw us, she clouded up and began to pout. "Don't wanna go, don't wanna go."

"Hush," I said, raising my hand as if to cuff her one good.

Nellie Straight rushed across the kitchen and grabbed my hand. "Don't you be hittin' that child. She's just gettin' better."

"I wasn't really goin' to hit her," I said. "Besides, I think she's gettin' spoiled as well as better."

July stuck her tongue out at me, and for a minute I knew how Longhair Jim felt about her.

July was still at Mrs. Straight's the day Sandy Peters and Judd Ambrose rode in. Dickey-bird, Sallie, and I were at the store, which was fairly crowded for us—maybe four, five customers at once—when they walked in.

Judd Ambrose was a tall, thin, awkward man. His hands dangled at his sides, his legs were like perpetually bowed toothpicks, and he walked just slightly bent over. Now, he had a worried look on his face, clear to be seen behind a scruffy mustache and the color put on his face by work outdoors.

They waited patiently until the store cleared out, and then Sandy said abruptly, "Miss McNutt, this here's Judd Ambrose."

Ambrose stood looking at the floor, the hat in his hands being worried into a circle by his turning the brim round and round. "Ma'am," he said nervously, "I worked for your cousin."

With Sallie you could always tell right away whether or not she liked someone. She hadn't liked Longhair Jim; she liked Judd Ambrose. "I know you did, Mr. Ambrose," she said in what I thought of as her friendly voice. "And you've been accused of killing him."

"Ma'am, we had some hard words between us, and I admit they was all my fault. I said some things I never meant to, but I was drinkin' then and not seein' the world clear. Best thing that happened to me was your cousin firing me. Made me look at myself one more time, and I went out to Sandy's camp where there ain't nothin' to drink. But I didn't kill Mr. McNutt. You gotta believe me." He looked like an earnest child, denying the theft of a penny candy.

"I do believe you," Sallie said. "You don't look like a killer."

"Ma'am, I never hurt nobody but myself," he said.

Sallie laughed, "And you're through doing that, am I right?"

"Yes, ma'am."

Sandy Peters broke in. "We came here first, but we got to go now to the marshal's office. Judd will have to clear his name."

"I'll go with you to speak on his behalf," Sallie said, and I thought to myself, Oh, no, we're gonna close the store again.

But she surprised me. "Lizzie, you're in charge while I'm gone. And both of you, have some lessons done for me when I get back."

We stood like soldiers at attention, saying, "Yes, ma'am," me so proud I would have burst the buttons off a uniform if I had really been a soldier. Sallie could sure make me look at myself when I'd been wrong, but she also really made me proud of myself at times.

I watched the three of them stride off toward the marshal's office, Sallie taking two steps to every one taken by the men, whose bootheels clomped on the wooden sidewalk, signaling their determination. One or two heads on the street turned as Sallie walked along with a cowboy on either side of her. In Fort Worth cowboys were a dime a dozen, but they didn't often have the company of a fine lady like Sallie. More than likely, you'd see them in the Acre with Lulabelle's girls.

At first, the rest of the day seemed a letdown. Sallie came back within an hour and reported that the marshal had believed Ambrose but there would have to be an investigation, and meantime Ambrose was free in Sandy Peters's custody. They would be staying in town a few days until everything was cleared up.

"Back to your lessons," Sallie said briskly, "and then the storeroom needs sweeping, Lizzie, and Dickey, the cooking utensils in the front window are dusty."

I sighed aloud. I wanted to solve the murder and free Judd Ambrose and keep Longhair Jim away from Sallie, not work on spelling and handwriting.

"By the way," Sallie said offhandedly, "Mr. Peters tells me he cannot imagine why the murder has to be solved before I can inherit the store and that wonderful big house with all its grand furniture."

I felt as if someone had stuck a knife through me. Sallie was still thinking of the house as it was when we first saw it, but only Ben Boy and I—and Walter Lambreth—knew that it was now nearly empty. How could I let her go on dreaming of those grand furnishings? But then, how could I break my word to Ben Boy and tell her the truth?

Before I could say anything either way, she went briskly on, "Now the spelling words for today are . . ."

"Can't we have a music lesson?" I asked with a grin. "You can sing 'Barb'ra Allen,' and we'll learn it."

"You already know it!" she retorted with a smile. "Spell 'merchandise.' It's a good word for people who work in a store."

The monotony of the day broke rather suddenly late in the afternoon when Walter Lambreth stormed into the store. "Miss McNutt! May I have a word with you?" Then with a glare in our direction he added, "Privately."

Sallie smiled sweetly. "Of course, Mr. Lambreth. You seem upset."

"Upset? You're right I'm upset. I've just learned that we have finally caught Stephen's murderer, and you, his very own kin, testified in the man's behalf!" His voice boomed so loudly throughout the store that the thought of privacy was ridiculous.

Dickey-bird and I simply stayed out of sight behind a stack of men's pants.

"Mr. Ambrose did not kill Stephen. I'm convinced of that."

"You're convinced of that," he mimicked. "And what, dear madam, makes you suddenly an expert in criminal justice?"

Sallie flared in anger. "I may know little about criminal justice, Mr. Lambreth, but I know people. I know who I trust and who I don't."

"I have asked you before to keep out of this and let me handle it. Now I must insist. I will—"

Before he could finish, Sallie broke in with a tone like ice. "Mr. Lambreth, I'll thank you to leave my store *now.*"

"Your store? Not yet, madam, not yet." He turned on his heel and marched out of the store, his face as red as the long underwear we sold.

I followed a few steps behind him and stood at the door watching him stalk away. And I grinned when I saw Ben Boy step out of a nearby doorway and follow Lambreth down the street.

We had just closed the store for the night and pulled down the shade in its glass panels when Ben Boy knocked. When I let him in, he was breathless from running.

"Mr. Lambreth," he panted. "I've . . . found something . . . out."

"Whoa," Sallie said, "sit and catch your breath before you try to tell us." She brought him a drink of water, and after a minute he seemed composed.

"Mr. Lambreth," he began. "I was following him, and he went to his office, and stopped and bought cigars, and then he headed for the White Elephant. But on the way, he met this man, I don't know his name, but he was dressed in a real nice suit and had a hat on his head and, you know, he looked like a rich man to me."

"Probably was," I said. "There's lots of them in Fort Worth."

"And an equal number of very poor children," Sallie murmured.

"Go on, Ben Boy," I urged.

"Well, I hid around the corner of a building where they couldn't see me, but I could hear them, and the man, he says to

Lambreth, 'I hear you have some furniture and carpet for sale.' Lambreth says, kind of low, 'That's right, I do.' And the man says that his wife sure would admire to have an oriental carpet in her dining room, and Lambreth says, 'I may have just the thing. It will be in my office tomorrow. Come by and look at it. And do bring your lovely wife.' "

"Lovely wife!" I scoffed.

"That's what he said, Lizzie," Ben Boy protested. "But don't you see? Remember that rug in Mr. McNutt's dining room?"

My heart sank, just as Sallie looked sharp at him. Here I'd been so careful not to betray Ben Boy's trust, and now he himself had given the secret away. As I said, sometimes I thought he needed a keeper.

"How do you know about a rug in Stephen's house?" Sallie demanded. "And what would that possibly have to do with a man wanting a rug for his wife?"

There was nothing for it but to confess our nighttime visit to the McNutt house. At first, Sallie was less horrified by our description of the empty house than she was by our breaking and entering the house and being on the streets in the middle of the night.

"You children have got to have some supervision," she muttered. Then, in a more normal tone, "Tell me about the rug."

We described it, and Ben Boy insisted it must be the one that Lambreth planned to sell.

"Maybe it's just a coincidence," Sallie said. "How could he possibly sell something out of Stephen's house?"

"Maybe he needs the money and doesn't care so much about right and wrong," I suggested. "What else could have happened to all that furniture?" It seemed to me that the conversation between those two unidentified deep voices, the conversation that Ben Boy and I heard from inside a closet, was a clear indictment of Walter Lambreth.

"Well, you'd need more proof than you have to accuse him," she said, but I could see that she was puzzled and disturbed, probably less by the thought of losing the furniture than by the dishonesty involved.

Ben Boy and I looked at each other, and I knew what he was thinking. "Yeah," I said to Sallie, "maybe you're right."

"Yes, ma'am," she corrected absently.

Eight

WILD ROARING was coming from Lulabelle's parlor by seven o'clock that evening, and two of her girls got into a brawl that spilled over into the street, with each of them brandishing a broken bottle and shouting terrible threats at the other. Ben Boy and I were used to such goings-on, and he just looked at me and said, "You can sure tell warmer weather's here."

But Dickey-bird was horrified and followed me like a shadow. When he heard that Ben Boy and I had to go out that night, he insisted on going.

"We got to get there 'fore dark," Ben Boy said, "and you just can't go fast enough."

"I will," he promised. "I'll run faster than you. You'll see."

"He'll give us away," Ben Boy protested in a darkly prophetic tone.

"Dickey-bird," I said, looking solemnly at him, "will you do exactly what we tell you, no matter what happens?"

"Cross my heart," he said with the appropriate gesture.

"Let him come," I told Ben Boy. "He may see something we don't."

It was close to sundown when the three of us set off for Samuels Avenue, and Ben Boy hurried us without mercy. "We got to get there and be hidden 'fore they come to steal that rug, and that could be anytime after dark. I want to look around first, too, and find the best hidin' place. I ain't hidin' in no closet again."

Dickey-bird looked puzzled, but I didn't feel obliged to tell him about the time Ben Boy and I almost got caught in Stephen McNutt's house.

The sun was going down to the west in a blaze of pink and orange and yellow streaks across the distant prairie when we turned north on Samuels Avenue, and by the time we got to the McNutt house, it was comin' dark. Ben Boy cussed our lateness, until I told him to shut up 'cause I wasn't listening to language like that.

"You been around Sallie too much," he spat.

I didn't point out to him that he was doing it because of Sallie. Ben Boy might have been doing it in part because he never could resist a daring adventure.

"Dickey-bird," he said, "see that bush? The one that's already green and thick, right near the front door? You get inside it, and you stay there without makin' a noise 'til I come get you, even if it's morning 'fore I do. Understand?"

Dickey-bird nodded solemnly, and we watched him crawl into the bush. Ben Boy surveyed carefully and decided he was well enough hidden.

"Listen to whatever they say, so's you can report it," he instructed. "Now, Lizzie . . ."

"Yessir!" I snapped, standing at attention.

"Cut it out, Lizzie. This is serious. You take the dining room window, but stay close to the side of the house, and stay quiet!"

"Where're you goin' to be?" I asked.

"Never you mind. I'll be around, but you won't see me."

We stayed in our positions probably a good hour with nothing happening except that it got inky dark out 'cause there was no moon. I'll give Dickey-bird credit—he never peeped, and I don't think that bush ever rustled.

Must have been close to nine-thirty when we heard a wagon approaching. Instinctively I froze in my position when the horses stopped at the gate of the house, but I couldn't see anything from around on the side where Ben Boy had stationed me. I strained my ears, but there was no conversation, just the sound of the gate opening and closing and heavy men's feet on the front verandah. Then someone lit the gas light in the dining room.

Even with the flame of the lamp, it was hard to see through the sheer curtain over the dining room window. I cupped my hands around my eyes and pressed my face so close to the window that it fogged a little from my breath. I could make out two bulky shapes, and one of them sure looked like Walter Lambreth! Then I heard muffled voices.

"That's it. Move that furniture off it. Here, I'll help with the chairs, but be quick now." Walter Lambreth was giving orders, and a man I'd never seen, I didn't think, was following them. He looked to me like someone Lambreth had picked up in a tavern in the Acre.

Lambreth must have thought so too. "Here, you oaf, don't bang that table. It's a valuable piece of furniture. Take a care!"

They got the table and chairs ringed around the edge of the room, and Lambreth ordered, "Now roll up that rug."

The other man bent to obey while Lambreth stood and supervised. I wondered where Ben Boy was and if he was taking all this in, but I kept watch as they rolled the rug, hoisted it, and left the room, with Lambreth stopping to put his end of the rug down long enough to brush off the gray gloves he wore and then turn out the gas. In no time at all, they were through the front door and down the steps off the verandah. I snuck silently to the edge of the house to peer around and watch.

And that's when it happened. Dickey-bird, hidden right there in that bush, not two feet from Walter Lambreth, sneezed. Not once, but twice, great loud sneezes that shook the whole bush. To me, it seemed they shook the whole earth. My heart leapt into my mouth, and my knees turned to jelly.

"What the hell . . . ?" the other man exclaimed. "You told me there wouldn't be no one here."

"There isn't supposed to be," Walter Lambreth muttered through clenched teeth, reaching into the bush where Dickey-bird, terror-struck by the enormity of his error, sat frozen until he was roughly hauled out by Lambreth. "One of those damn Acre brats!" he exclaimed, holding Dickey-bird so tight by the back of his collar that the poor thing was struggling for breath. "I'm tempted . . ." He let his threat dangle.

"What the hell?" the other man repeated. "What's this young un' doin' here?"

Lambreth was silent a minute, as if thinking, and then he said clearly, "No doubt staking the house out for his friends to come and loot it. Isn't that right, young man?"

"N-n-n-noooo," Dickey-bird stammered.

"Don't lie to me," Lambreth ordered. "I think we'd best report this to the marshal. Here," he said to the other man, "you get that rug in the wagon. Then you can hold him, and I'll take the reins. We'll dump the rug and then take this brat to the marshal, where he'll get what he deserves."

I drew my breath in silently, thinking how scared Dickey-bird must be and how he really couldn't take care of himself. Ben Boy would have kicked Lambreth once where it hurt and been gone before either man could think. Ben Boy? Where was he? I turned my attention from the men, one now struggling with the rug, which really needed two men, and the other with Dickey-bird, who offered no resistance but just stood there shaking. Out of the corner of my eye, I saw Ben Boy creeping along the edge of the fence, in plain sight if those two had ever thought to look. But they were busy.

"Lambreth? This here boy's goin' to tell about the rug, and then the whole thing's up anyway."

"Nobody'll believe him, an Acre brat," Lambreth said smoothly. "He and his friends will get the blame for this rug and the other things missing in the house. Just do what I tell you. I'm not paying you to think."

I stiffened in indignation. Lambreth was going to frame us for stealing all that stuff out of the house. Ben Boy sure better have a good plan now.

Ben Boy crept up next to me, motioning for silence, and together we watched helpless while they threw first the rug and then poor Dickey-bird into the back of that wagon. The name-less man climbed in with Dickey-bird, and he must have given his arm a sharp twist for good measure from the sound of the wail that came from Dickey-bird. Lambreth took up the reins.

They weren't out of sight when I turned to Ben Boy. "Where were you?"

"In the wagon," he said miserably, "under a cover. I was gonna go along and see where they took it. Had a dickens of a time climbing out 'fore they saw me."

"What do we do now about Dickey-bird?"

"I don't have any idea." He shook his head miserably.

Of course what we did, no matter the hour of the night, was run to Sallie. It must have been near ten o'clock when we banged on Nellie Straight's front door. That good woman finally came to the door muttering, "Hush, now, a body'd think some-body was being killed. What's all this racket in the middle of the night?" She opened the door and peered at us through sleepy eyes.

"Lizzie! What in heaven's name . . . ?"

"Sallie, Mrs. Straight. We need Sallie right away. It's . . . it's real important." We had run, and I was hard put to catch my breath.

Sallie appeared magically behind Mrs. Straight. She was in a high-necked nightgown with a robe thrown over it and her hair no longer swept up but falling loose around her shoulders. Somehow it made her look less grown-up and efficient and ca-pable, and my heart sank. What made us think Sallie could do anything?

"Dickey-bird," I panted. "The marshal's got him."

She flared in anger. "What were you children doing? I told you not to be out on the streets at night!"

"Wait a minute," Ben Boy broke in. "We did it for you."

"For me?"

And then the whole story came out, in bits and pieces and no kind of order, and Sallie and Mrs. Straight sat spellbound listen-ing to us. While Mrs. Straight breathed an incredulous "Walter

Lambreth!" Sallie put her chin in her hand, a gesture I had learned to recognize as her thinking position.

"Let me get dressed," she said finally, without giving us a clue as to what was in her mind. She was gone only a very few minutes, and when she came back it was obvious she had dressed hastily. Still, she looked more able to deal with the world than she had in a nightgown.

"Where're you goin'?" Mrs. Straight demanded.

"To the marshal's office, Nellie. We must. You watch July for us, please."

Nellie sniffed. "As if that little one weren't already in my care. Folks trampin' off in the middle of the night . . ." Muttering to herself, she headed for the back of the house.

I was made a little nervous by Sallie's plan. What if the marshal decided instead of letting Dickey-bird go he should throw Ben Boy and me in jail, too. "Sallie? Maybe we should wait here . . . or at the shack."

"Of course not, Lizzie. I need you to explain to the marshal. Come along, now."

If I thought Ben Boy hurried us earlier in the evening, it was nothing compared to the pace Sallie set now. We were at the marshal's corner of the courthouse basement in no time at all.

An angry-looking deputy sat behind the desk, and Sallie spoke directly to him. "I understand you arrested a young boy tonight."

The man carefully eyed Ben Boy and me until I wanted to shrink out of sight. Finally, he turned to Sallie. "That's right. He's back there with a couple of drunks from the Acre. Want me to put these two with him?"

"No, I do not!" Her tone was indignant. "I want you to free that boy immediately."

He got up slowly and walked around the desk. "Well, now, ma'am, I can't rightly do that. He stole something. And I reckon these two were part of it."

I turned to leave but Sallie reached out and grabbed my wrist.

Without looking at me at all, she said, "These children stole nothing. They were witnesses, however, to thievery."

He laughed arrogantly. "Yeah, Mr. Lambreth told me they'd say that. Well, it's their word against his, and I reckon I know where the marshal's sympathies are. It ain't with brats from the Acre."

Sally's face turned deep red in anger. "They are not brats . . ."

"Ma'am," Ben Boy interrupted softly, "we best go now."

Sallie paused in mid-sentence, stared at Ben Boy, then whirled to face the deputy again. "Not until I see Dickey."

"Your choice, ma'am. But I can't change his quarters just 'cause you don't like them."

Dickey was indeed in a jail cell with two other men, one of them sprawled on his back on the floor, snoring loudly and oblivious of anything around him. The other was a sometime card dealer I'd seen often enough in the Acre. He watched impassively and never gave a sign that he knew us.

Dickey huddled miserably in a corner, his face buried in arms bent across his folded knees. When the deputy hollered at him, he raised a tear-stained face and saw us. I've never since seen any living person look happier to see someone than Dickey was to see us that night.

"Lizzie! Ben Boy! And Miss Sallie . . . you've come to get me!" And then he paled and turned somber. "Ben Boy, you mad at me?"

"Naw, Dickey-bird. I guess a body can't help a sneeze." It was said without much conviction. Ben Boy would never have allowed himself to sneeze.

Sallie took charge. "Dickey, we can't take you with us tonight. But I'll think of something first thing in the morning. Are you all right until then?"

Dickey's thin little body seemed to deflate with disappointment. He looked at the hard floor of the jail cell. "Yes, ma'am. Don't worry about me. It's more important to get that rug back."

Impatiently, Sallie said, "Dickey, you're more important than

any rug, but I cannot do anything until morning. Do you understand?"

"Yes, ma'am," he nodded.

"I don't 'spect morning's gonna make no difference," the deputy jeered as we left.

"Lizzie, Ben Boy, you'll have to see me back to Nellie's and be
there again early in the morning. You'd best just curl up in the
parlor."

"No, ma'am," I said. "We'll be back early in the morning."

And we were, after a fitful night of fretting and tossing and
playing "What if?" in our minds.

Though Ben Boy and I were bedraggled from lack of sleep,
Sallie was bright and business-like. Dressed in her gray voile
with the chiffon bow at the neck and an ever-so-tiny gray hat to
match, she sat at Nellie's big old dining table sipping coffee. July
sat next to her, contentedly spooning a bowl of oatmeal. One
look at me and she began her new refrain of "Don't wanna go
with Lizzie, don't wanna go."

"Hush, July," Sallie said absently, while I threw the child the
dirtiest look I could manage. Ben Boy and I sat almost motion-
less over the bowls of oatmeal that Mrs. Straight served us. We
were sleepy, worried, and, in the back of our minds, angry at a
world that permitted such injustices as Dickey-bird's capture
and Walter Lambreth's escape.

"Lizzie," Sallie said. "Sit up straight and don't lean over the
table. You, too, Ben Boy."

Resentfully, we both obeyed. Table manners were never a
central concern with us and certainly not now.

"I'll go with you to open the store," Sallie said, "but then I'll
be gone awhile. I'm going to see Mr. Paddock at the newspaper."

"Why?" I asked suspiciously.

"I think it's time the people of Fort Worth knew how some
children are treated within their city, and Dickey in jail will
make news."

"Will that get him out?" Ben Boy didn't care about larger social causes, but he wanted Dickey-bird to be free.

"It might," she said. "Lizzie, I hate to leave you alone in the store, but I want Ben Boy to find Mr. Peters and tell him what's happened. Then, Ben Boy, I'd like you to stay with Lizzie until I return, or at least set up your shine box in front of the store."

Ben Boy just nodded, not too pleasantly, but I asked, "What about Longhair Jim? You goin' to tell him, too?"

"I imagine he'll find out," Sallie said, dismissing the idea of seeking the gunfighter out.

Find out he did. Longhair Jim came storming into the store just after Sallie had left for the newspaper office. It was the first time I'd seen him of late that he didn't smell of whisky. I guess that was because it was still early in the morning.

"You brats are making things worse by the day," he bellowed. "Now that what's-his-name bird or something is in the hoosegow."

I felt like telling him we already knew, but I was quiet until he pushed me too far by saying, "Trying to steal McNutt's furniture! Of all the dumb . . ."

"We weren't trying to steal nothing!" I shouted.

"Aha, so you admit you were there too!"

Ben Boy had come up behind Longhair Jim. With his fists clenched as though ready to fight, he came around to face him. "Yes, we were both there. And we found out something you should have found out in your so-called investigatin'."

"Likely," Jim said sarcastically.

I wasn't sure I wanted Ben Boy to tell everything he knew, but it was too late. "Did you know Walter Lambreth is stealing the furniture out of Mr. McNutt's house?"

The startled look on Longhair Jim's face was a clear answer that he did not know. He recovered quickly enough to say in a patronizing tone, "Of course I knew that. I'm setting a trap for him, but you kids may have ruined everything now."

"Better spring your trap 'fore that house is completely empty," Ben Boy said disgustedly, turning away.

"Yeah," Jim said. "But you kids keep out of my business or . . ." His threat dangling, he turned and marched out of the store.

"I'm leavin'," Ben Boy said. "I got to find Mr. Peters and then I think I'll see what Mr. Lambreth is up to."

So there I was, alone in the store while everyone else was off solving Stephen McNutt's murder and getting Dickey-bird out of jail. In frustration, I banged my hand down so hard on a glass display counter, it's a wonder I didn't shatter it. It was a long morning for me.

Sallie came in toward dinner, with a midday meal in a sack for me and a much larger one she intended to carry to Dickey-bird at the jail. "We thought I'd better take something for those other men, or Dickey wouldn't get to eat what we brought him," she explained.

"How's July?" I asked as she headed out the door.

"Fine, just fine. And Mr. Paddock's going to be a big help. I'll tell you all about it when I get back." She was gone again, and I was resentful. The day dragged on, with few customers and nothing happening, except that Ben Boy came in to report that Mr. Lambreth was spending the whole day in his office, apparently conducting business as usual and acting as though nothing had happened. I told him to see if he could get close enough to the window to see if the rug was in there, but he looked at me like I was dumb.

"You don't have to tell me, Lizzie. I tried. Can't do it right now."

Toward mid-afternoon, Sallie returned, obviously disturbed. "Poor little Dickey," she said. "He's just miserable in that jail. Hungry and dirty and frightened, most of all. The only bright note is that Judd Ambrose has been arrested."

"Why is that a bright note?" I demanded. "He didn't do anything."

"Oh, I know that, but he and Dickey are in the same cell, and he's good company for Dickey. The sheriff said Mr. Ambrose either has to be cleared beyond a doubt or stand trial."

I doubted that Judd Ambrose would consider that a bright note, and I wouldn't blame Sandy Peters for feeling his plans had gone astray. My day had certainly gone astray, and I was beginning to feel like a caged animal, with everyone else making plans and doing things and me just helpless.

"I got to go," I mumbled, heading for the door.

"Lizzie, whatever for?" Sallie had just settled at her desk. "I haven't even told you about Mr. Paddock yet."

"I'll hear it later," I flung over my shoulder and ran out before she had a chance to stop me.

Spring had arrived in Fort Worth, and it was a sunny, bright day, not too warm, and just enough breeze stirring to feel good. I wandered absently toward the courthouse, as though standing outside would help Dickey-bird. I never would have gone in for fear they wouldn't let me back out. The Acre breeds a fierce fear of any form of the law.

After staring at those stone walls for a long time, I drifted over to a spot on the edge of the bluff where I could sit and look out over the prairie. Directly below me, the bluff was tangled with brush, and here and there a redbud bloomed brightly. In the distance, I could see spots of bright color on the prairie—the first spring wildflowers were blooming. The world looked so pretty to me that I wondered how it could go so wrong—Dickey in jail, Mr. Lambreth stealing all Stephen McNutt's things, the murder not solved. It suddenly appeared to me that no one else was doing anything right. Longhair Jim, Ben Boy, even Sandy Peters, and most of all Sallie—they were muddling around in circles and not getting anywhere.

Sometimes there's a moment when you see things so clear that it pretty near scares you. That moment happened right then to me, and I saw, plain as day, that I would have to do something. I was losing control of the world, and I needed to get it back. The first thing would be to get July and take her to the shack where she belonged.

I jumped up and ran for Mrs. Straight's, pounding on the door when I got there. "Mrs. Straight, July's better now, and I got to take her home," I poured out, still panting from my run.

"Land's sake, Lizzie child, calm down a minute. She's better, and it's probably best you take her. I got new boarders and so much cooking to do I can't see the next day ahead."

So far so good. I had expected an argument. My determination strengthened, I rushed into the kitchen, where July sat playing in a patch of sunlight on the floor. Her dark hair was combed and she wore a pretty yellow ribbon in it, matching the little yellow dress Mrs. Straight had made for her. It made her copper skin glow, and she looked healthy and happy.

Until she saw me. "Don't wanna go with you, Lizzie," she shouted.

I picked her up roughly, shook her once, and said sternly, "I'll box your ears if you say that once more." Then I felt guilty. But, to my surprise, she never even whimpered while she got together her few things, mostly what Mrs. Straight had given her, and she said her goodbyes, hugging Nellie Straight so tight I thought they'd both burst.

"We're obliged," I said awkwardly. "You saved her, and I'll . . . well, I'll clean your house free ten times."

"Go on with you," Nellie said. "No call to do that. I did what I could. When I need it, you'll do the same for me."

July followed me home, struggling to keep up with my fast pace. "Lizzie, you're walkin' kind of fast," she said tentatively.

"We got lots to do, July. Dickey-bird and Sallie both need our help."

I expected a wail, but she just gave me a long look, and then she nodded, as if she understood.

The shack was messy. Ben Boy and I had only run in and out since Dickey-bird was arrested, and it showed. I had begun to sweep and straighten and think about what I could fix for dinner, and July had gone outside, "to show Lulabelle to her dolls," she said, when Chance came storming in, waving a newspaper.

"Have you seen this?" he demanded.

"Hold it still long enough for me to tell," I said crossly, never pleased to see him.

"Your precious friend has really done it this time." His loud voice, raised in outrage, brought July in from the street.

If I thought July would cling to my skirts, like she always did, I was wrong. "You leave Lizzie alone," she stormed, standing in front of Chance with her hands on her hips, in a pose that obviously echoed Nellie Straight's stance.

"Get away from me," Chance growled, still waving the newspaper.

"It's all right, July," I said, reaching a hand for her and automatically pulling her behind me. My attention was riveted on the newspaper with the words "children" and "outrage" in the bold black headline. "No," I said, turning away, "I haven't seen it."

"Here, let me read it to you," he shouted angrily. "The headline says, 'Lives of children in Acre an outrage,' and it goes on to talk about how the good people of Fort Worth should be ashamed that children are living in their midst in such conditions, and it describes your shack—no names, of course, but its plain to identify. Lulabelle's pretty easy to spot too. Then it says that one of these pitiful children now languishes—that's the newspaper word—in jail in the company of known drunks."

"Dickey-bird!" July wailed, while I, stunned, could think of nothing except how hurt Lulabelle would be. She'd think I ratted on her.

Chance read on until I thought he'd never stop. "Mr. Paddock is calling for an all-out effort on the part of everybody in Fort Worth to close the Acre."

My heart sank. Close the Acre? "They can't do that."

"Yes they can, Lizzie, and Miz McNutt is going to be the one to blame. They can close all the saloons and places like Lulabelle's and even tear down this shack if they want to."

"Where would we go?" I asked, frightened at the prospect.

"Who knows? I don't think they thought that far. And it's all because of that snowbird you took in."

"All because of a sneeze," I said absently, thinking about how things happen in a chain. If Stephen McNutt had never been murdered, and if Sallie hadn't ridden on the same coach with Longhair Jim, and if Dickey-bird's father hadn't left him on a street corner, then Fort Worth would have kept its eyes closed to the Acre.

"What? What kind of nonsense are you talking?"

"Nothing," I said. Somehow I'd lost my taste for cleaning the shack. "Read it to me again, Chance."

It sounded worse the second time he read it.

"Lizzie?" July said, as Chance disappeared out the door, "I won't leave you." Her warm little hand crept into mine, as though to comfort me.

Nine

BY MORNING, I knew what I had to do. I'd lain awake most the night figuring, and I had sorted out what was most important and what had to be done. The most important things, it seemed to me, were to get Dickey-bird out of jail and to stop Mr. Paddock from drawing attention to the Acre. And to do that, we'd have to prove that Mr. Lambreth was stealing Stephen McNutt's furniture. Along the way, we might solve the murder, but it was low on my list.

Ben Boy was still sleeping when I began bustling around the shack. He raised his head and opened one sleepy eye. "What're you doin'?"

"I got important things to do today. Ben Boy, I got to trap Mr. Lambreth, I just got to!"

"That's Longhair Jim's job," he said, stretching. "Me, I got to shine some shoes today."

How he could think of shining shoes at a time like this was beyond me. I threw a dress on July, though she was barely awake, grabbed her doll, and headed for 'Phronie's kitchen.

" 'Phronie, you got to keep July for me this morning. Please?"

"Land, Lizzie, I ain't go no time for that child."

"It's important, 'Phronie. The whole Acre might depend on it."

"What you gonna do now, Lizzie?"

"You'll see. You just keep her. I'll tell Lulabelle."

I hurried to knock on Lulabelle's bedroom door. When she

called softly for me to come in, I burst through the door, asking her if 'Phronie could keep July and telling her how sorry I was about the newspaper article, all in one breath.

"Relax, sweetie," she said. "It's happened before, it'll happen again."

"But, Lulabelle, if they close down the Acre, where will everybody go?"

"There's always another town, Lizzie. Always thought I'd admire to see San Francisco. Maybe that's where I'd go."

"Aren't you worried about it?"

She yawned. "Not me, sugar. I got better things to worry about. Now run along and tell that old witch in the kitchen to bring my breakfast."

I flew back through the kitchen, where July had now come full awake and was eating toast that probably had been intended for Lulabelle.

"Go Mrs. Straight's now," she said, looking directly at me.

"You will not, July," I said sternly. "Thanks, 'Phronie. Lulabelle wants her breakfast." And I was out the door.

Sallie was the next stop on my list, and I was still early enough to catch her at Mrs. Straight's, or so I thought. Actually, I met her walking away from the boarding house. The package in her hand made me think she was probably headed to see Dickey-bird before she went to the store.

"Lizzie! Whatever brings you out so early?"

"Lots of things. Sallie, I ain't goin' to the store this morning. I . . . I got some important things to do."

She frowned at me. "What could be more important than getting Dickey out of jail? I wanted you to talk to Mr. Paddock yourself this morning. He said he'd be at the store."

I almost screamed and kept from it only because the streets were already busy with farmers come to town to trade and merchants getting ready for another day. If I'd screamed, I'd have attracted a huge crowd. "Sallie, don't you see? You've got to stop him, you can't let Mr. Paddock write these things about the Acre."

"Lizzie, he must, it's his civic duty. The citizens must be alerted to the situation that exists in their city."

"How many businessmen do you think don't know about the Acre?" I asked disgustedly. "They know. Lots of them own property there. Others come there to gamble and drink . . . and even meet ladies. They know, Sallie, but they don't want to be reminded in the newspaper."

"I want you children out of there!" She stuck her chin out in determination. "You don't have a chance to make use of whatever abilities the good Lord gave you. You'll . . . you'll end up at Lulabelle's . . . or something worse."

"There's lots worse," I admitted, "and I'd like to live somewhere else. But I got responsibilities . . . and friends, like Lulabelle."

We had reached the courthouse, both talking so hard that we'd hardly paid attention to where we were going. I went in with her to say hello to Dickey-bird and tell him not to worry, though it took some courage on my part to face that deputy who wanted to jail Ben Boy and me the other night. He was at the desk again and made some smart remark about Sallie bringing another of "them damn brats" to get free room and board in the jail. July'd have stuck her tongue out at him, and I nearly did 'cept Sallie put a hand on my arm as if to hold me back. All I did was glare.

Dickey-bird was in much better spirits than the last time I'd seen him. "Mr. Ambrose has been tellin' me all about bein' a cowboy, and I reckon I'd like to be one," he said happily.

"Boy's right smart, he is," Judd Ambrose said, grinning shyly. "Me and him, we get along good."

Sallie was right. Judd Ambrose had an open, honest face and sure didn't look like the killer kind. Well, if my plan went through he'd probably go free. Dickey-bird and I talked for a minute, and I told him not to worry, though with Sallie right there, I couldn't tell him what my plan was. I tried to wink to give him a clue, but all he did was ask me if I had something in my eye. Dickey-bird and Judd Ambrose deserved each other, I decided.

The clock on the jailhouse wall told me it was getting on toward the opening of business hours. I had to hustle. "Sallie, I'll see you later in the day at the store. Dickey-bird, you be good, and don't worry." I ran out before Sallie could stop me.

Walter Lambreth had probably not yet arrived at his office on Houston Street, a short, quick walk from the courthouse and jail. I wished desperately that I had kept that one good dress Sallie gave me instead of being so high and mighty and leaving it at Mrs. Straight's, but it was too late now for second thoughts. Straightening my old cotton dress and my hair as best possible with my hand, I went in to confront Lambreth's clerk.

"Is Mr. Lambreth in?" I acted as dignified as I could, but I knew there was no hiding what part of town I lived in.

"Not to the likes of you. Never will be." He was a thin, spindly young man with wire-rimmed glasses and a scraggly moustache. Ben Boy could have whipped him with one hand behind his back.

"Mr. Lambreth is expecting me," I said, sailing past him to the inner office.

"Wait! You can't go in there."

"Mr. Lambreth is expecting me to talk about the matter of breaking Stephen McNutt's will," I said loftily. "I have important information for him." That mollified the young man a bit.

"Well, if you say McNutt, but I still bet you two pennies Mr. Lambreth will throw you out on your ear."

I ignored him and settled in a wingbacked chair, facing the desk and not the door, so at first glance Lambreth wouldn't see me, not that the weasel of a clerk wouldn't tell him I was here. Then I began to look around the office. Sure enough, rolled along one wall was the carpet from the McNutt house. The carpet on the floor was another of intricate oriental design, and I remembered the missing carpet in the parlor of the house. There was a fancy desk with a leather top and papers scattered carelessly behind it. And in one corner of the room stood a good-sized safe.

I must have sat there half an hour, getting more nervous as the time went by. I had rehearsed what I would say, but my mind seemed unable to hold on to the phrase and more than once I was tempted to climb out a window and be gone. After all, I had seen what I needed to—the carpet—and I could go to the marshal's office with my find. But that deputy was there, and without Sallie's protection, I might end up right next to Dickeybird. No, I had to wait.

Finally I heard that too hearty voice say, "Good morning, Gibson," and the clerk responded, "Good m-m-morning, sir. Ah, there's something . . ."

But Lambreth, obviously in a hurry, brushed by him and strode into the office, going directly to the safe, where he bent down and began to work the combination. I sat still as a mouse, but the clerk came to the door, still stammering. "Uh, Mr. L-l-lam . . ."

"Not now, Gibson, I have important matters on my mind."

Gibson gave up and I stayed quiet, watching fascinated while Lambreth removed stacks of money from the safe, along with what looked to me, who'd never been inside a business, like legal papers. At last, he whirled to his desk and saw me.

"You!" he shouted in a rage. "What are you doing in my office? How dare you? Gibson! Gibson!"

I opened my mouth to reply, but the sentence I'd rehearsed froze in my mouth, and Gibson, meantime, recovered his tongue. "She—she said she had to talk to you about Mr. McNutt," he told the glowering lawyer. "I thought it m-m-might be important."

You could really see Lambreth thinking for a long, silent minute, and then, in a changed tone, he said, "McNutt, eh? Yes, yes, of course, I'll talk to the young lady." I squirmed uncomfortably in my chair at that. "But Gibson, I'll need you to run some errands for me. I want you to take these papers"—he grabbed the nearest stack—"to Lawyer Davidson's office and be sure he reads every word of them. Don't leave until he does. And then go to the courthouse and trace the ownership of this parcel of land." He picked up another sheet of paper.

"Yessir," Gibson said, "but, sir, that's liable to take me all day."

"I understand that, Gibson," Lambreth said patiently, "but you will be doing important work and I'll make do without you."

The bravado I'd mastered coming into the office was leaving me, slipping away bit by bit, until I reminded myself of what Ben Boy would have done. He'd never have sneezed in that bush as Dickey-bird did, and he'd never let fat old Lambreth bully him as I was about to. I stiffened my backbone, but I did wish that Gibson person wasn't leaving me alone with Lambreth. I sat in silence and Lambreth fiddled with some papers until we both heard Gibson call, "I'm leaving now," and close the door behind himself.

Lambreth's attitude changed again, right quick. "All right, you brazen hussy, what do you want to tell me about Stephen Mc-Nutt?"

I took a deep breath, prayed for confidence, and plunged in. "That you're selling the furniture from his house and cheating Sallie, and that you probably killed him. I have the proof— eyewitnesses."

He looked startled for just a minute, and then he blustered, "A passel of Acre brats! No one will believe you."

"I've left proof with Sallie," I lied. "You're trapped, Mr. Lambreth." I added that latter with much more confidence than I felt, thinking I'd have to remember to tell Ben Boy how proud he'd be of me.

"I doubt that," he said drily. "I've got a few aces up my sleeve."

I thought it particularly appropriate that he used the gamblers' description of cheating. "You know it's over," I told him. "Now that we all know, there's no way you can sell anything else out of the house. And you'll have to pay Sallie for what you've sold."

"Pay her, my foot!" he exploded, without realizing that he was, in a way, confessing.

"Longhair Jim Courtright is on your trail right now and about to find out everything."

"Longhair Jim!" He fairly spat the words out. "He's a drunken has-been and nobody in this city listens to him." He reached down into a drawer and straightened, leveling a pistol at me. "Now let me tell you how we're going to solve this," he said.

I sat still in the chair, a feeling of unreality creeping over me. For all that I'd seen in the Acre, nobody had ever held a pistol on me before. For just a moment, panic surged through me, as I wondered if I was going to die, sitting right there in that chair. Sure would make a sensational headline for Mr. Paddock's article about the Acre, I thought wryly. But then I realized Lambreth couldn't possibly shoot me here in his office and explain it satisfactorily to the marshal.

"You won't shoot me," I said with more confidence than I felt. "Somebody would hear, and your clerk knows I am with you."

"Right," he said smoothly, "I won't shoot you, but you and I are going for a carriage ride. You're my safe passage out of the city. If you behave, nothing will happen to you, though heaven knows I'd be justified in putting a bullet right between those conniving eyes of yours."

I tried to stare calmly at him, but my mind was whirling. Once Walter Lambreth was out of town, he'd be scot free but his guilt would be obvious, Dickey-bird would be released, Sallie would get her house, and life would go back to normal. Wasn't that all I wanted? Another look at Lambreth convinced me that wasn't enough. I couldn't, I just couldn't let him get away with all he'd done.

"You did kill Stephen McNutt, didn't you?"

He looked long and hard at me. "What does it matter? Of course I did. I asked Stephen for a loan to cover my losses at the White Elephant—Short was pushing me to pay. But Stephen turned preacher on me and refused, giving me a lecture on gambling instead, so I killed him right there in the store. He'd earned a lot of money over the years at that store—an incredible amount, really—and with him dead, I had control of his estate because there were no heirs. The receipts at the store, the fine furnishings he'd indulged in, all his property was mine. It all went all right until that woman showed up.

"By the time you get anybody to believe your story, I'll be on my way to New York City, with a satchel of money, and you . . . Well, now that you've figured out the truth . . ." He let his threat dangle.

I gripped the arms of the chair, my knuckles turning white, and wished for Ben Boy to get me out of this. The trouble was I'd thought I was so darn smart by not telling anyone, not even Sallie or Ben Boy, where I was going. Maybe if I reminded Lambreth that no one would believe me anyway . . . but something kept me from begging for anything from such an awful man.

"You just sit there while I gather some things," Lambreth said. He kept the gun always in his hand, and he rarely turned his back on me for more than a second as he shoveled money and papers into a satchel.

"I've been planning my trip for some time, waiting for the right moment," he said, all of a sudden seeming to take great pleasure in telling the story. "You've made today the right moment, and I'm indebted to you."

"Mrs. Lambreth?" I asked.

"Ha, she'll never miss me. She has money of her own, and her life will go right on. The old battleaxe. The girls at the White Elephant will miss me more."

Fat chance, I thought, feeling sorry for Mrs. Lambreth, whoever she might be.

"My carriage is right outside," he said. "We'll walk to it, you slightly in front of me and carrying, uh, this stack of papers." He grabbed another stack.

"Won't people think it's funny—you and me together?" I asked, clutching the papers to me as though they were a shield.

"Not really. I've used Acre brats before to run errands. One named Chance . . ."

"Chance Coker," I supplied.

"That's the one. You know him? Of course you do. Fine fellow, knows how to survive. I admire that."

I'd have even been grateful to see Chance at that minute, but it did strike me as somehow fitting that Lambreth and Chance had done business with each other.

"Now," he said, "up out of the chair, and walk slowly out of the office. My pistol is in my pocket, hidden but handy."

It seemed ten miles from the chair to the door, but far too soon we were out on Houston Street. Men pushed by us, some tipping their hats to Lambreth, a few looking curiously at me, but none stopped.

"Wait," I wanted to cry, "can't you tell he's going to kill me?"

I thought of Sallie and the whole long chain of events that had led to this moment, and I wondered why any of it had seemed so important. Stephen McNutt's furniture, even Dickey-bird's freedom, weren't important enough to die for.

"Into the carriage," he said. "I'll walk around the other side, but don't try anything."

I calculated my chances and found them poor. The carriage top was rolled back, and I would be out of his sight for no longer than two seconds as he circled behind. Not long enough to loosen the reins, and besides, I had no idea what to do with a harnessed horse. My chances for escape lessened with every move away from his office.

"Lambreth!" a vaguely familiar man's voice called out suddenly.

"Courtright!" Lambreth said, the surprise in his tone obvious. Instinct sent me tumbling to the floor of the carriage. Longhair Jim never went unarmed, and he probably still had a tendency to solve disagreements with gunfire, in spite of his sinking reputation—maybe more so, in fact.

"Pull the pistol out of your pocket real slow and throw it down," Courtright ordered.

"Pistol? Now, Jim, I have no such thing . . ." Lambreth tried to sound friendly and surprised. He only succeeded in sounding nervous.

"Do as I say, *now."* Courtright's voice was like iron.

"All right, Jim, just be slow . . ." The words were cut off by the blast of a gun. Two more shots, and then silence, as if the whole world had suddenly become stone quiet. I huddled on the floor, afraid to get up, until I felt a hand grab me and heard Longhair Jim's voice.

"You can get out of there now. What fool thing were you trying to do?"

My knees were weak and I wanted to hug Longhair Jim, who would have hated that. Shakily I said, "I was tryin' to solve Stephen McNutt's murder . . . and get Dickey-bird out of jail."

"Hell of a way to do it," he said contemptuously.

I walked around the carriage and saw Lambreth sprawled on the ground, still clutching his satchel in one hand and a pistol lying loose near the other hand. "Is he . . . ?"

"Dead," Longhair Jim said. "I guess you did the city a favor," he added grudgingly.

I looked again at the man who had murdered and caused so much trouble, and then I fainted, dead away.

Next thing I knew I was at Mrs. Straight's, with Sallie and Ben Boy and July and Sandy Peters and Longhair Jim all standing around me while Mrs. Straight waved smelling salts under my nose.

"Lizzie?" Sallie asked, dabbing at her eyes with a handkerchief. "You're all right."

"Yes, ma'am," I whispered, somehow afraid to talk louder.

"I told you she was fine," Courtright said in his usual tone of disgust.

"Wow, Lizzie! You did it, you trapped Lambreth!"

"But I didn't mean to get him killed," I wailed. "I didn't want anybody killed."

"It was him or you," Courtright said tersely. "I knew that when I went looking for you."

"You went looking for me?" He was my hero, after all, I thought.

"I told him to," Ben Boy said excitedly. "After you left it dawned on me what you said, and I got scared. So I found Longhair Jim, and then I went for Mr. Peters."

"But it was all over when I got there," Sandy Peters said. "Marshal was taking the body away."

"The marshal!" I exclaimed, my voice returning to normal. I sat up shakily. "Dickey-bird? Where is he?"

"Still in jail," Sallie said. "The marshal's waiting to talk to you, but there should be no problem. Lambreth had a whole lot of money with him and papers that incriminated him in Stephen's death and the theft of things from the house."

So we went to the jail and got Dickey-bird and Judd Ambrose out of jail, and then all of us—even Longhair Jim Courtright— went back to Mrs. Straight's and had one of her big roast beef dinners in celebration. And in the middle of the celebration, Longhair Jim raised his glass in a toast. Mrs. Straight had given him just a drop of her homemade apple brandy.

"To Stephen McNutt," he said. "May he rest in peace."

And we all said, "Amen," as though we were praying. Sallie had a tear in her eye, but she smiled when she caught me looking at her.

And I looked at Longhair Jim and somehow, just for a second, I didn't see the rumpled suit and the bleary eyes—I saw the man who had saved me. When I looked again, he looked shabby and a little afraid, and it made me sad.

I thought that was the end of it. Life would get back to normal, or as close to what it used to be as possible. Sallie'd move into the McNutt house, and we could settle down in our shack again where, if it wasn't always comfortable, it was familiar and safe. Dickey-bird and I would still go on working for Sallie, and Ben Boy would drift in and out between shoeshines, but Walter

Lambreth was gone from our lives, and Longhair Jim would have no need to be hanging around Sallie anymore.

I had it all wrong, which shows how little I knew about the world. First of all, there was the house.

"I'll have to get another lawyer," Sallie mused even as we sat at the dinner table that very night.

"Why, ma'am, I just happen to know the very one," Longhair Jim said, a trifle too quickly.

"Thank you," she said in her sweet voice that meant she was ignoring him, "but Mr. Peters has already kindly put me in contact with a reputable gentleman."

By the look on Sandy Peters's face, I knew that was a bald-faced lie, but I figured Sallie, like me, had had enough of Longhair Jim Courtright.

He humphed and harrumphed, and pretty soon allowed as how he'd better be going. Sallie was effusive in her thanks as she walked him to the door, but I saw Jim turn and give Peters a long, hard stare. It came to me so sudden I almost said something aloud—Longhair Jim'd make trouble for Sandy Peters, if I didn't do something about it. He was that jealous of Sallie.

"Shoot," Sandy laughed soon as the door was closed, "I ain't never had a lawyer. Don't even know enough to know when I need one. But if it'll help you, Sallie, I'll go find one."

"I know," Sallie said, "but I figured I didn't really trust any lawyer Jim Courtright recommended."

Mrs. Straight, of course, knew just the perfect lawyer, and that matter was solved.

July began to yawn pretty soon—the excitement having gotten the best of her—and she near knocked me to the floor when she said, "Lizzie, can't we go home now?"

I eyed her suspiciously. "July? You aren't gonna make a fuss for staying with Mrs. Straight?"

The child threw Nellie Straight a huge smile and said, "No, Lizzie, I want to go home with you."

I was flattered, even though I should have known better, and began to round up Ben Boy and Dickey-bird for the long walk home. It was Dickey-bird who objected, shadowing as close to Judd Ambrose as he dared.

"Aw, Lizzie . . ."

"Dickey-bird," I threatened, "you come on now. Mr. Ambrose has had his fill of you."

"No, ma'am, I really haven't," Judd Ambrose said. "I . . . I like Dickey-bird's company. I'll be sorry to be leavin' him."

Dickey-bird gave him a long look. I could see him screwing up his courage until finally he said, his voice quavering, "You promised!"

Ambrose blushed, looking plain uncomfortable. "Later, Dickey," he said, as close to gruff as he ever came, "later. I got to talk to Mr. Peters."

Crestfallen Dickey-bird headed out the door and would not even have thanked Mrs. Straight for dinner if I hadn't yanked him back with a sharp call. Then, with prompting, he managed a mumbled thank-you, but it looked to me like he was about to cry.

Ben Boy was scornful on the way home. "Thought jail would've toughened you up some, Dickey-bird," he said. "Guess you'll never learn."

Dickey-bird surprised him with a well-aimed kick to the shins. "Shut up, Ben Boy! You don't know what you're talkin' about."

Before I could holler "Stop!" they were on the ground, poundin' on each other, and it took all the kickin' and pullin' I could do to get them apart. "You two stop it right now," I commanded. "What do you think Sallie would say if she saw you actin' this way?"

Dickey-bird was quiet, but Ben Boy scoffed. "Sallie this, Sallie that! We acted this way before she ever came along, and you never said nothin'."

Dumbfounded, I opened my mouth to give Ben Boy what-for, until I realized I couldn't deny what he said. My ideas about how people behaved had changed a whole lot since Sallie had come into our lives. I didn't used to think much about fighting . . . and now it seemed to me a dumb way to settle problems.

"Just shut up and come on," I muttered, not ready to admit this new vision aloud.

July took my hand and swung along beside me. "They're naughty, aren't they, Lizzie?" she asked.

But it dawned on me that she hadn't been behind my skirts all day, not even when Longhair Jim was around, nor when the boys fought.

"Can't you walk faster?" I asked roughly. It didn't look to me at all like things were going to get back to normal, and I was almost scared.

I was really scared two days later when Sallie announced she was moving into the McNutt house the next day. It wasn't that she was moving, it was the way she put it.

"We'll be moving into the house tomorrow," she said. "Now you children must gather your belongings, and I'll have a wagon come for them."

At first I started to laugh at the idea that we had enough belongings to need a wagon. But then, the truth of what she said sunk in. "Why do we have to gather our belongings?" I asked slowly.

As though it were perfectly obvious, she said, "Well, you can't possibly let me live in that big house alone, can you?"

"Yes, ma'am," I said, "we surely can. We belong in the Acre."

"Nonsense," she said impatiently. "Just because Nellie Straight thinks I shouldn't give you ideas above yourselves doesn't mean I'm going to leave all of you to wallow in that shack while I rattle around in a huge house alone. You're coming to live with me."

"No, ma'am," I said emphatically. "We can't be beholden." I didn't mind being beholden to Lulabelle, 'cause it wasn't much beholden anyway, but this was different. The balance would never be equal, and then Sallie would have the right to act like a parent. I'd had a dose of that from her and didn't like it at all. No, it was less my honor than my independence that I feared for.

"I'm going to live in the house," July announced, going to stand by Sallie.

"July!" I said, raising my hand. "You'll do as I say."

"You aren't my mother, Lizzie," the ungrateful child said, sending a sharp pain through me. I may not have been her mother, but I'd raised her and I expected more gratitude.

Sallie grabbed my upraised arm, her voice as sharp as I'd ever heard it. "And that's another thing, Lizzie. I won't have you treating July that way. Physical punishment accomplishes little."

"It gets her attention," I said, "when she's being a spoiled brat."

"Lizzie, Lizzie, I've so much still to teach you," Sallie said, shaking her head.

I turned away angrily. I'd already learned enough that threatened my way of life. I didn't want to learn any more.

"Move into the house!" Ben Boy said in amazement when I told him Sallie's plan. "I will not! She'd have me bathin' every day and probably even goin' to school."

"And she'd never let you go out at night," I said darkly.

"And we'd have to eat vegetables," he said. "No, Lizzie, the shack is ours, and we ain't goin' nowhere."

"Aren't going anywhere," I muttered, before I realized that I was sounding like Sallie.

Dickey-bird listened to our conversation silently and then said, "I think you ought to go. I'm goin' to live on Sandy Peters' ranch with Judd Ambrose."

"You what?" we both echoed incredulously.

"You heard me," he muttered. "I'm goin' to live on Sandy Peters' ranch."

"Just like you to leave us," Ben Boy said disdainfully. "I knew you weren't tough enough for the Acre."

"It ain't that," Dickey-bird said. "I just want to live with Mr. Ambrose. He reminds me of my pa. And I don't suppose I ever want to be tough enough, Ben Boy."

Amazement spread over Ben Boy's face, for being tough was the supreme virtue to him. And, until recently, to me.

A part of me ached to live with Sallie in that big house. It was better than Nellie Straight's, more than I'd ever dreamed of. And deep down I came as close to loving Sallie McNutt as I had anybody save maybe July. But give up the only way of life I'd ever known? The place where I'd learned that no matter what else I could take care of myself? Trade that for unknown dangers, unseen threats?

"I ain't goin'," Ben Boy whispered in the dark after we'd all settled down for the night.

In the end, I packed his clothes, along with mine and July's, while he was off shining shoes.

Ten

DICKEY-BIRD got his wish and flew away to Sandy Peters's ranch. Sallie was not pleased.

"He'll get no schooling," she said.

"I'll teach him," Sandy promised. "You give me the lessons, and I'll see that he does them. And we'll report to you, say every three months."

"You'll teach him?" She arched her eyebrows to emphasize the question.

"Went through the tenth grade," Sandy said calmly. "Just don't show doin' the kinds of things I do now."

"I don't want to do book-learnin' kinds of things either," Dickey-bird chimed in, but Sandy cut him short with a stern look.

"I'll see that he studies," Sandy promised, "and besides, it'll give me an excuse to come back to town more often." His tone said plainly that he meant an excuse to see Sallie, and she softened.

"I'd like that," she said, so low I near blushed that I could overhear it.

Judd Ambrose spoke up tentatively. "I can't teach him no readin' and writin'," he said, "but I'll see he gets some useful learnin', like ridin' a horse."

Ben Boy's eyes widened, as though he was thinking of going too, and I kicked him when I was sure Sallie wasn't looking. I couldn't have borne it if Ben Boy deserted me.

"I'm sure you'll be a help to him, Judd," she said. "And Dickey, we'll miss you." Sallie did what I'd never have dared to do—she reached over and hugged Dickey-bird.

He squirmed a little bit and looked at the floor, but he managed a muttered "Thank you . . . I'll miss all you too."

"Yeah," Ben Boy managed. "Bet you'll toughen up on a ranch." His tone was wistful, and I hated him for even thinking of going.

"Don't fall off no horses," I said as casually as I could. I figured Dickey-bird shouldn't mean much to me, newcomer that he was and all, and I couldn't understand why I felt so bad.

July had no doubts, though. She flew across the room to bury her head in his stomach, about where she reached on him, and wrap her arms around him. "Dickey-bird," she wailed, "don't want you to go."

Without a touch of embarrassment, Dickey-bird stroked her head and said softly, "I'll bring you a present, July."

She raised a tear-streaked face. "I'd like a horse."

We all laughed, and Sandy told her he didn't think that was possible, but they'd bring something special.

And then they were gone. Dickey-bird was out of our lives, and it was me, Ben Boy, and July again. Except now Sallie was in charge, not me.

Ben Boy had pretended to be angry when he found his belongings removed from the shack. Sallie'd been all for going to the Metropolitan to tell him but I warned against that.

"He'll come looking for us," I assured her.

"It's a long walk," she protested.

"Weather's nice," I said unfeelingly.

Nice weather or not, Ben Boy was indignant—and hungry—when he arrived at the McNutt house late that night. "Might tell a body when you're takin' his belongings," he said.

"You wouldn't have come," I replied calmly, cutting off a piece of steak for him and heaping his plate with fried potatoes. Ben Boy hadn't eaten that well five times in his life, I bet, and the food silenced all argument.

When he saw his room—his very own room all to himself—
he whistled low and said, "Wow! You sure I don't have to share
this with Lizzie and July?"

"No," Sallie laughed, "that's not quite proper, old as you boys
and girls are. The girls are in a room across the hall."

He never said another word about going back to the shack, at
least not that day.

Our room looked out northwest, across the prairie, and sometimes offered us spectacular sunsets. But at night, with the moon
still to the east behind us, it was inky dark out there, and July
was scared.

"Sleep with you, Lizzie," she said.

"No, July, you sleep in the trundle bed like Sallie said." I was
firm, and she curled into a ball, soon asleep.

Me? I never told Sallie—and I'd have threatened July if she'd
woken up and seen me—but I put my blankets on the floor for
more than a week. Much as I longed to sleep in a bed, I couldn't
somehow get used to it. Finally one night, I swore I'd stay in that
bed all night, even if I lay awake till morning. Once I'd made up
my mind to it, I slept soundly and Sallie had to call me three
times that morning.

"Sleepyhead," she teased. "You'll let the whole day slip away
while you lounge in bed." And then she was off to the kitchen,
singing about a poor, wayfaring stranger.

I had to admit that I was glad to be in the McNutt house, at
least some of the time.

"Is Mrs. McNutt here?" A dignified lady, dressed fine, had
come into the store. She didn't look to me as if she needed the
kind of thing we sold—saddles and such—and I wondered if
she was trouble.

"Yes, ma'am," I said, remembering Sallie's training. "I'll fetch
her."

Sallie followed me out of the storeroom, her hand extended in
greeting. "I'm Sallie McNutt."

"I'm Mrs. Walter Lambreth," the lady said, and my heart sank.

"Oh, Mrs. Lambreth," Sallie said, "I'm so sorry about your husband."

The *Daily Democrat* had carried the story of Mr. Lambreth's death, saying that Lambreth and Courtright had a shoot-out and Mr. Lambreth lost. I was mentioned as a witness, though my name was not given—once again I was an Acre brat, though this time they substituted the words "apparently homeless child." Most folks assumed that the disagreement had to do with the railroad strike and Buttermilk Junction and that I'd just been there by accident. No one—not me, not Sallie, not even Longhair Jim—wanted to change that general opinion.

But it was soon apparent Mrs. Lambreth knew better. "Well," the lady said with amazing practicality, "I am sad and I'm not. But I want to thank you for coming to the funeral."

Sallie had gone, though she said she stayed in the back— there was a fine crowd of substantial citizens—and she forbad us to go, curious as we were. "It wouldn't be proper," she said.

"I . . . I wanted to speak to you, but there was such a crowd . . ." Sallie seemed more at a loss for words than I'd ever seen her.

"It's all right," Mrs. Lambreth said. "I understand more about my husband than most people think . . . and more than a lot of people in this city do." She glanced at me.

"Lizzie is the girl who was there when Mr. Lambreth was shot," Sallie said.

The large brown eyes widened. "Oh, you poor dear! I'm so sorry you had to go through that."

"It wasn't nothin'," I said, and then received a sharp look from Sallie, so I added quickly, "anything. I was just glad Longhair Jim's bullets didn't hit me."

Mrs. Lambreth even smiled a bit. "I'm glad too. I guess we'll never know what caused the trouble"—I looked deliberately at the floor—"but I wanted you to know that I was aware for some time that Walter was, ah, into things better left alone."

Sallie and I were both speechless, and I was remembering

what Lambreth had said about his wife—an "old battleaxe." She hardly looked or acted the part to me.

"I came . . . because Walter had brought some things home that I suspect belong to you, Mrs. McNutt."

"Things?" I'd never seen Sallie so dumbfounded.

"Yes. A lovely mahogany secretary, and an English oil painting, and some dishes. I want to return them."

"Oh, Mrs. Lambreth, keep them and enjoy them," Sallie said.

"I'd never enjoy them," the lady answered, her tone briefly harsh. "They belong with you. And the fewer memories I have, the better off."

Walter Lambreth was some awful man, I thought.

Before Sallie could reply, the bell over the door jingled, and we turned to see none other than Longhair Jim Courtright walk into the store. He strode deliberately up to Sallie.

"Got important things to talk to you about," he said curtly, ignoring Mrs. Lambreth. "Found out some of your stuff is in Lambreth's home."

Sallie's stare was furious. "Mr. Courtright, this is Mrs. Walter Lambreth."

He was taken back only momentarily. "Good day," he said, bowing slightly. "I assume you know you have stolen property in your home?"

"Mr. Courtright," Sallie said, her tone icy, "we can handle this without your intervention."

He looked startled. "Well, now, what did you hire me for . . . ?"

"I *didn't* hire you!" Sallie replied vehemently.

"Well, you sure as shootin' need my help, ma'am, trusting as you are." He shot a meaningful glance at Mrs. Lambreth, but she, with true dignity, saved the whole situation.

"Mr. Courtright, I do have some things that belong to Mrs. McNutt. If you would be good enough to see to their transfer, I'd be sure that you were, ah, rewarded."

"Certainly, ma'am, certainly. Glad to do whatever I can to help."

Arrangements were made, and Courtright and Mrs. Lambreth soon left. The minute they were out the door, Sallie began to stomp around the store in anger.

"That man!" she said, more loudly than she was wont. "He's got to leave us alone! The very nerve . . ." She picked up a whole pile of shirts and threw them, one by one, on the floor.

July wordlessly rushed to pick them up and began refolding them.

"Sallie," I said somewhat tentatively, "he's trying to sweeten you . . ."

"He's a married man!"

"That doesn't bother him," I said, and then I remembered how she and Sandy Peters looked at each other. Longhair Jim had made another of his classic mistakes.

July took to living in Sallie's house like she'd never lived in a shack. Within days she was taking a hot bath every night, eating stacks of pancakes for breakfast, and running around behind Sallie to do everything she could to help.

"Sallie, I can sweep the kitchen floor," she'd say proudly, and Sallie would hand her the broom and never say a word about the crumbs and dust she missed. Me, I'd have blessed her out and told her if she was going to sweep a floor she might as well do a right good job of it. But Sallie just hugged her and said how proud she was.

And Ben Boy—he took to soft living too, quick as a sponge takes to water. Wasn't long before I noticed he wasn't out the door first thing in the morning, shoeshine box in his hand. One morning it was near ten o'clock when I caught him eating eggs and bacon in the kitchen. Sallie had gone to work but left breakfast behind warming and drying out in the oven of the wood-burning stove.

"Ben Boy, somebody else'll get all your shines today," I sang out maliciously.

"Don't matter, Lizzie. I don't got to bring you potatoes and stolen apples and fifty cents for dinner." He smiled at me smartly.

"Ben Boy, we can't be takin' advantage of Sallie. We got to earn our keep," I said ferociously.

He turned smug. "Sallie thinks it's more important for us to eat right and get plenty of sleep and exercise." He stretched like a show-off, and I near boxed his ears.

"Ben Boy . . ." I didn't know where to go with my threat, but I sure knew I was serious.

"Don't get in an uproar," he laughed. "I'm gonna shine shoes today. And you and July are gonna work in the store, just like always. The world ain't changed, Lizzie, 'cept it's got a little easier."

I wasn't sure.

"Lizzie?" Sallie sat at her desk in the store, figuring her endless accounts. "You seem awfully unhappy, and it's bothering me. Can we talk about it?"

"It's nothin'," I lied, picking up the broom and starting to sweep with a vengeance.

"I'm grateful I'm not a spider on that floor," she commented. Then, grabbing the broom from me in a gesture most unlike her, she said, "Lizzie, if we don't talk and straighten this out, it's all for a waste."

"What's all for a waste?" I asked, puzzled.

"You and me and Stephen's house and everything I've tried to do since I've been here."

"Why?" I didn't mean to be dumb or difficult or anything like that, but what I heard her saying was that everything she had done was for me to approve, and I couldn't take that responsibility. "I can walk away from here today," I told her, "and you'll still have all that you wanted."

She gave me a long, hard look. "No," she said, "I won't. Because you're a big part of that."

"I ain't . . . am not . . . your responsibility. Nobody hoisted that off on you. Not Ben Boy nor July either."

"No," she said slowly, "nobody foisted that off on me. But I took it on . . . because I wanted to. And you are my responsibility, at least if you'll accept that." She twirled the ink pen in her hand so that I was afraid ink would fly around the room at both of us, and she studied me so hard that I was forced to look at the floor. "Lizzie, what's the matter?"

It was the most direct question anyone had ever asked me, and I was hard put to answer it. "I'm not sure," I muttered. Then, as though the words came out of me in a rush, I said, "I always thought if Ben Boy and July and I could get out of that shack, I'd be the happiest person alive. But it ain't like that. Ben Boy, he ain't in a rush to go shine shoes. And July . . . she don't whine so much, but she don't listen to me either. And she never tries to crawl behind my skirts no more." My grammar, which had much improved under Sallie's influence, seemed to go backward, and I was vaguely aware of it.

"Any more," Sallie said. "You're feeling like they don't need you now that they have me, aren't you?"

Indignant, I yelped, "No, it ain't that!"

"Think about it, Lizzie . . . are you sure?" She never took her eyes off me, never gave me the chance to escape. Before I could answer, she went on, "Lizzie, without you, these children probably wouldn't have survived at all. You did something so important that I can't even begin to describe it. But if you help me, I can do more for them. I can get them out of the Acre."

I stared at her, then at the floor. That was what I wanted for all of us—out of the Acre. But I guess I thought I had to do it for us, not have somebody else whisk us up and save us. Don't ask me, with a ma like I'd had, where I got that notion of having to earn your future yourself.

"Don't you see, Lizzie—if you hadn't given Ben Boy and July the strength you have, I wouldn't be able to help them. They'd be locked forever in the Acre. But because you've cared for them, I can help them."

My mind went back to basics. "July don't mind me at all," I said petulantly.

Sallie almost laughed, and I saw her stifle the impulse. "Is that what's bothering you? And is that what you want? Remember, if July minds you, she also always hides behind you. I think she's growing up a bit."

"If I can't raise July, what can I do useful?"

Sallie laughed aloud then, and she did something nobody had ever done. She simply came toward me and threw her arms around me. "Lizzie Jones, there are a thousand things you can do useful, here and at the house. You don't need July to make you important."

Now Nellie Straight had rubbed her hand across my back in a gesture of affection from time to time, and Ben Boy had grabbed my hand once in a while, and of course July had curled against me in the night, but no one, not since I could remember, had ever hugged me just outright as Sallie was doing. I had to pull away, almost rude, because I feared I was going to cry.

Sallie never said a word—she just stood there, watching me go, and that night at supper, she said, "Lizzie, why don't you cook tomorrow? Ben Boy and July are used to your cooking, and I'm sure they'd welcome a meal."

I made stew and apple cobbler, and bless them, they all ate heartily.

Late March was the finest time of the year in North Central Texas, at least to my mind. The redbud began to show its deep purple-pink color, peach trees put forth a faint pink that grew each day, and wildflowers turned the prairie a bright yellow— we could see it from the upper windows of the house. If we'd been closer, we'd have seen the deep shade of bluebonnets and the brightness of Indian paintbrush mixed in occasionally, but from a distance it was all the color of sunshine. I loved walking from the house to the store, looking at the new pale green on the trees and smelling the air. Everything was making a new start—even me.

"Lizzie? You're singing!" July looked at me in amazement as we walked up Samuels Avenue. "You sound like Sallie!"

"And how does Sallie sound?" I asked.

"Happy," was the reply. And pretty soon July was trying to sing about Barb'ra Allen, too. We were both off-key and unsure of the words, but we didn't care.

Sallie had never mentioned our talk again, but I'd noticed that she'd send July to me for help most of the time, instead of taking care of whatever it was herself. "Lizzie, Sallie said to ask you to button my dress," or "Lizzie, write my name for me so's I can copy it."

Ben Boy got a little better about getting out to get shoes shined. "Got to get back on the streets," he said to me confidentially one evening. "Now that we're so far away, I don't know nothin' that's goin' on, and that ain't good."

"I guess not," I said slowly, uncertain whether the goings-on in the Acre still affected us but reluctant to cut all ties. "How's Lulabelle?"

"Not so good," he said. "One of her girls took real sick, like to died, and that kind of stopped folks from goin' there. Lulabelle's talkin' about movin'. Says she can still see a reform comin', whatever that means."

According to Ben Boy's reports, things weren't going well for Longhair Jim either. "Standing guard at the White Elephant, he is," Ben Boy said one night.

"Standing guard?" Sallie asked cautiously.

"Throwin' out troublemakers, stoppin' fights, that kind of thing," Ben Boy said. "A bouncer."

"A bouncer!" Sallie looked as if she'd just understood. "Why didn't you say that to begin with?"

"I didn't know you'd understand what I meant," he laughed, ducking as she tried to cuff him lightly.

"I'm not that protected," she said. "Sometimes you children seem to think you're to take care of me, instead of the other way around."

"Maybe," I said softly, "it's a bit of both."

Sallie laughed, "Maybe so, Lizzie, maybe so." And she went off into the kitchen, singing about the wayfaring stranger.

We didn't see Longhair Jim, either at the house or the store, for a long time. I 'spect he was embarrassed that the detecting business was not going well and that he was reduced to working for Jake Johnson and Luke Short at the White Elephant. None of us missed him, though, and as time went by we didn't even mention him.

But we missed Dickey-bird, and the day Sandy Peters walked into the store, Dickey-bird in tow, was one of great celebration.

"Herd's out west of town," Sandy said. "We came on in to get supplies and, of course, to visit."

Not so many trail herds actually went through Fort Worth these days. As the railhead in Kansas moved progressively west, so did the trails, and lots of herds waded the muddy Red River at a place called Doan's Crossing, northwest of Fort Worth by a good bit so that their line of travel took them beyond the city. The bosses still came in for supplies most of the time, for there wasn't another city close by to provide flour and sugar and coffee, but we didn't see many cattle in town.

"You goin' to Doan's Crossing?" I asked, proud that I was so knowledgeable.

"Nope," Peters said. "We're goin' the old way, gonna come right through town. Not a big herd this year," he added, "only about fifteen hundred head."

"Fifteen hundred cows? Through Fort Worth?" Sallie was horrified.

"Sure," I said, still puffed with knowledge. "They used to all the time. Down Rusk Street, right through the Acre, and then over to Samuels and down to the Cold Spring crossing."

"Down Samuels Avenue?" The look of horror on Sallie's face intensified. "Past our house?"

Sandy laughed. "We may be the last herd to go that way, Sallie. Be a real experience for you. You can stand on the front porch and watch us go by."

"And watch them trample the flowers and break down the

fence," I added cautiously. I didn't want to make Sandy Peters angry, but I knew about trail herds through town.

"Now, Lizzie," the tall cowboy said, "we can manage our herd better than that."

"Yeah," Dickey-bird said. "I'm gonna ride that paint pony tied out yonder."

His whole attitude was changed. The frail, scared Dickey-bird had been replaced by a kid who walked cocky, talked like he had something to say, and didn't act like he'd mind me if I told him to do anything. I wasn't at all sure that Sandy Peters had done Dickey-bird a good turn.

Dickey-bird was, though. He obviously adored Peters and barely took his eyes off him, looking for approval with almost every gesture he made and word he spoke. And Sandy Peters was generous with his approval.

"You're goin' on the drive?" I asked incredulously, just as Sallie said, "Oh, I don't think he should. Dickey-bi . . . ah, Dickey better stay here with us."

Dickey-bird looked like he was going to howl, but Sandy said, "Stuff and nonsense. This here's a good sidekick, and I need him on the drive."

Dickey-bird like to burst with pride. Sallie looked doubtful, and Ben Boy and I were both green with envy.

"Are you here for supplies?" Sallie managed to ask, between Dickey-bird's loud and lengthy descriptions of life on the ranch.

"Well, that, and to take you to dinner, I hope" was the answer. "Thought Dickey might stay at the house with the others while you and I went to Peer's House. I got a room in a hotel so I could clean up and all."

I hoped she was impressed that Sandy had gotten a hotel room. I bet he'd even get a shave 'fore he came to take her to dinner.

"I'd like that," Sallie said, looking like she was indeed impressed.

And so, I got to cook dinner again that night, while Sallie dressed in her made-over gray silk dress. I'd watched her weeks before as she slimmed down the skirt, added a tucked satin vestfront and some leaf-shaped appliqués, and generally made a new dress out of an old one.

"There," she'd said, biting off the thread, "no one will ever know this dress is ten years old."

"But where will you wear it?" I asked. It was far too fancy to wear to the store, and that was about the only place Sallie ever went.

"I'll find someplace," she said, and began to sing about Barb'ra Allen.

Ben Boy came home while I was flouring steak to fry. The kitchen was a mess and hot besides, and my temper was short. Much as I wanted to cook and be in charge again, I'd gotten myself into a mess of dirty dishes and sputtering grease.

"Lizzie!" he shouted from the back door. "Lizzie!"

"Ben Boy, what's the matter with you?" I asked crossly. "I got to fix dinner and can't be bothered with you yelling at me." It felt good to holler at him that I was busy—like old times.

"Where's Sallie?" he asked suspiciously, still clutching his shoeshine box.

"She's upstairs dressing. Sandy Peters's takin' her to dinner tonight." I felt very important giving him this news and followed it with a kind of "I told you so" look which was completely lost on Ben Boy.

"That's what I'm tryin' to tell you," Ben Boy said.

"What? You haven't tried to tell me a thing."

"Shhh." He lowered his voice to a whisper. "Longhair Jim. He says he's out to get Sandy Peters."

"Out to get Sandy Peters?" I yelped.

"Lizzie, could you please whisper? I don't want Sallie hearin' this." Ben Boy was disgusted with me.

"What do you mean 'out to get'?" I asked, my voice appropriately low. I shook the flour off my hands as best I could and wiped them on my apron, creating a dust of powder which made Ben Boy cough.

"What do you think I mean?" he answered disgustedly, once he got his voice back. "We can't let Sallie go to dinner with Sandy. Longhair Jim, he knows Peters is in town, and he says he's not gonna let him leave."

"Why not?" I couldn't believe this. Of course I knew that Longhair Jim was jealous of Sandy and the way Sallie looked at him—hadn't I been the first to notice that?—but to think he'd challenge him to a shoot-out . . . Longhair Jim had gone 'round the bend for sure this time.

"He's puttin' out some cock-and-bull story about Peters and Judd Ambrose really havin' something to do with killing Stephen McNutt, and how Peters is now trying to get Sallie's fortune. But I think it's like you said, Lizzie."

"Like I said?"

"Longhair Jim's sweet on Sallie, and he doesn't want competition."

"Whew!" I drew a long breath. Ben Boy was right, and we had a real problem. No one could outdraw Longhair Jim, and surely not Sandy Peters, who probably didn't even carry a gun. "Was he drunk?" I asked.

"Is the sky blue?" was the answer.

So, drunk, Longhair Jim might draw on Sandy even if he didn't have a gun. Sandy could get killed, Sallie could get hurt, and even if she didn't, she'd never be the same again, seeing the man she loved—well, I thought she was beginning to love him —gunned down in front of her. And all because Longhair Jim was dumb enough to think Sallie'd ever look at him.

"We got to do something, Ben Boy," I said.

"Yeah. But what? I been thinkin' on it all afternoon, and I can't come up with a plan. We best just tell her not to go to dinner with him."

"We can't do that," I said. "Sallie'd never believe us . . . and Sandy'd be insulted that we thought he couldn't take care of himself and Sallie . . . and we just can't, Ben Boy." Then I added as an afterthought, "Dickey-bird's comin' for supper, while Sandy and Sallie go out, but he won't be much help."

"I think better on a full stomach," Ben Boy said pointedly, so I put the skillet back on the stove.

I'd never seen Sandy Peters in anything but Levi's and chambray shirts, but he surely did look fine when he pulled up to the house in a rented carriage that night. He had a black suit, not near as rumpled as that long-coated one Longhair Jim always wore, and he'd bought himself a new Stetson at the store that day, a fine felt hat. He still looked a cowboy, but he also looked a gentleman, and I could tell Sallie was impressed.

We said our good-nights, amid instructions from Sallie about getting July to bed and cleaning the kitchen—you'd think I'd never taken care of things before!

While I said, "Yes, ma'am," Ben Boy poked me hard in the ribs. "What the . . . ?"

"Shh," he commanded. Then as soon as they were out the door, he said, "I thought you were gonna stop them."

"Stop who?" Dickey-bird demanded. "Why?"

"Nothing," I muttered to him and threw Ben Boy a dark look. "I couldn't stop 'em. And neither could you," I added significantly.

"Lizzie," July asked, "what're you and Ben Boy talkin' about?"

"Nothing," I said shortly. If I hadn't been so worried, I'd have been pleased. Ben Boy and I were once again in the midst of an intrigue, sharing secrets and danger only with each other. But this intrigue had too much at stake—Sallie—and it wasn't old times in the Acre at all. This was too real.

We sent July to bed, but Dickey-bird refused to leave, and so the three of us sat huddled in the parlor, waiting to hear the sound of horses' hooves at the gate. Time inched by, and Dickey-bird's efforts at conversation didn't help at all.

"What's the matter with you two? Why don't you tell me what's goin' on?"

"Nothin'," I said shortly.

"I ain't that dumb," he said indignantly. "And Sandy says it's best always to be honest with people."

We sat, and we paced, and we waited . . . and it was only nine o'clock. They'd been gone two hours.

"Maybe I should go up to Peer's House," Ben Boy said.

"You gonna spy on Sandy and Miz Sallie?" Dickey-bird asked indignantly, but Ben Boy just gave him a dirty look.

"Yeah," I said, "maybe you should. I . . . I've got to stay here. . . . No, I can't stay here. I'm goin' with you."

Dickey-bird looked like we were talking in a foreign language. But he finally managed to say, "I'm goin' too."

We both turned on him. "No, you're not!" we said in chorus. Then I added, "You've got to watch July. Dickey-bird, this is important. Please do what I say."

He looked doubtful, so I added, "You're the only one I could trust with July."

That puffed him up a bit, and so he said, "All right," even if it was a mite reluctant. Ben Boy and I didn't wait; we were out the door before he could say another word.

The day had been warm, more like summer than spring, but with the sun gone the air had a March chill about it, and I was glad when Ben Boy urged me to run up Samuels Avenue as it climbed toward the city. Huffing some, we reached Belknap and turned west, toward the center of town. The streets were empty, 'cept for an occasional carriage that went by, and one drunk who demanded, "Where you kids goin' this time of night?" We brushed by as though we hadn't heard, and he settled back into muttering to himself.

"Where are we goin'?" I asked. "Peer's House or the White Elephant?"

"Peer's House," he said. "If Jim don't ever come near them, then we don't care where he goes."

"Sallie'll skin us alive if she finds us spying on them," I volunteered cheerfully. "And if she finds us out on the streets at night."

"She won't ever know," Ben Boy said with too much confidence.

Eleven

WE ROUNDED THE CORNER by Peer's House, talking to each other and not paying good attention to our surroundings. A month out of the Acre had made us soft, let us forget some of the caution that had sustained us all our lives.

Belatedly, Ben Boy grabbed my arm and whispered, "Look!"

There went Longhair Jim, into Peer's House as big as day. We were too late!

"Now what?" I asked disgustedly. "They won't let us through the front door of that hotel, and even if they did, I don't know what we'd do."

"I don't either," he said miserably.

But we kept on walking and in a minute we were in front of the windows of the Peer's House dining room. Curtains hung from a big brass railing halfway up the window, so we could stare into the dining room without being caught.

As we stood there, holding our breath in anticipation, we saw Sallie and Sandy Peters in one corner of the room, laughing and looking at each other like there weren't nobody else in the whole world. Sallie looked happier than I'd seen her since she'd come to Fort Worth, and Sandy, why he looked about to bust his buttons for joy.

And then, there came Longhair Jim stalking through the door, headed right for their table, though he wobbled a little as he walked. Ben Boy grabbed me, and I held his hand tight, but it was like we were watching a pantomime in slow motion. We had to just stand there and witness it, 'cause there wasn't a thing we could do. Worst of all, we couldn't hear.

Longhair Jim approached their table, and I could see a startled look on Sallie's face, even as Sandy Peters rose and offered his hand. Jim fanned the hand away, and drew back his coat—showing off those double holsters, I knew.

"Lizzie?"

"Yeah, Ben Boy, he's offering to shoot it out with Sandy."

We grabbed each other tighter.

Sandy Peters stood and swept back his own coat, plainly showing that he was unarmed. Then he raised his hands in a kind of shrug. Sallie, for that split second all this had taken, was sitting staring at the two of them, as though she didn't believe what she saw.

And then Sallie McNutt rose to her full height and faced Longhair Jim Courtright. She wasn't as tall as he was, but then she wasn't too far from it, and she'd put herself square in front of him so that she was speaking directly into his face. I wished mightily that I could hear what she said.

Sandy Peters, still standing, was staring at Sallie as if he'd never seen her before, and Longhair Jim had let his hands drop to his sides, his coat now covering those guns. The more Sallie talked, the more he began to back away, ever so slowly. As he inched backward, Sallie moved forward, following him, almost chasing him from the dining room, and talking all the while a mile a minute. Far as I could tell, Longhair Jim never did get a word in edgewise.

And suddenly, with Ben Boy and me still clutching each other, it was over. Longhair Jim was headed through the lobby of the hotel, and Sallie went back to her seat.

"We best get out of here *quick,*" Ben Boy said, pulling on my arm, and we turned to run.

Too late! A slurred voice behind us threatened, "Ought to draw my guns on you brats! What the hell you doin' spyin' on me?"

I would have turned to look but Ben Boy almost jerked my arm out of the socket, saying, "Run, Lizzie, run."

And so we ran, fast as we ever had in our lives, fully expecting to hear a bullet whine past us . . . or feel it sink into our backs. When we finally rounded the corner back onto Belknap Street and sank into a convenient doorway, I was shaking so hard I thought my teeth would rattle loose. Ben Boy couldn't talk either, and we sat there until our panting breath and shivering bodies quieted. Longhair Jim must've gone the other way.

"We best get home in a hurry," Ben Boy finally said, "less Sallie beats us there."

And so, once more, we ran. But this time it felt good to run again—Sallie had backed Longhair Jim down, and we were running home with the sure knowledge that she and Sandy Peters were just fine. The world looked good. Besides, we ran downhill much of the way.

Dickey-bird met us at the door, holding July by the hand.

"I woke up, and you were gone," she complained.

"Where've you been?" Dickey-bird asked.

"Nowhere," we both responded. "Quick, up into bed, everyone."

"I don't even have a bed here," Dickey-bird said, but we hurried him into Ben Boy's room.

By the time Sallie and Sandy came home, we were all peacefully asleep—or at least pretending.

Sallie's voice would have wakened the dead. "Imagine the nerve of that man," she said, before they even hit the front door.

"Now, Sallie," Sandy said more softly—I almost had to strain to hear him—"he wasn't himself."

" 'Course he was," she said angrily. "He was drunk, and Longhair Jim Courtright is never more himself than when he is drunk."

Sandy laughed aloud. "How'd you ever get mixed up with him?"

"I rode on the wrong carriage into Fort Worth," she said bitterly. "And now I can't get rid of him."

"He's sweet on you," Sandy said, "and I can't say I blame him."

"He's a married man!" She repeated the indignant words she'd said to me days earlier.

All Sandy said was "Glad I'm not."

July howled, and that gave us all an excuse to get out of bed and head downstairs. Rubbing my eyes, as though awakened from a deep sleep, I said, "What's goin' on?"

And Sallie spit out the whole story, never even thinking to scold us for being up late or anything. "That Courtright man . . . he . . . he threatened Sandy. Right in the dining room of Peer's House."

It was all I could do to keep from telling her that we knew that and would she please get on with the story. Ben Boy was a better actor than I'd ever be. "Threatened?" he asked innocently.

"Wanted to go outside and have a duel," Sallie said.

"Duel?" Ben Boy asked, as if the word was foreign to him, which it probably was.

"Shoot-out," Sandy volunteered. "Offered to meet me on the street. I didn't have a gun, and that took him back some . . . and then Sallie, she took him back a whole lot further." He grinned as he said it, and I thought Sandy was a pretty special man not to be threatened by having a woman defend him.

"What'd you do?" I asked, curiosity about to make me burst.

"Well," she said, still indignant, "I told him exactly what I thought of him—from his horning in on Stephen's murder to his disgraceful behavior toward his wife and daughters. Said I never wanted to see him in the store again, or in this house. Told him the murder was over and done with and solved, and our lives were going on, and he wasn't to upset them."

Sandy shook his head. "I never saw a gunfighter bow to a tongue-lashing before," he said, "but she whipped Courtright sure as she'd held two pistols on him. He just backed away, and never said a word."

There was a long silence while we digested this, and I couldn't help but think it was the saddest thing that ever hap-

pened to a gunfighter. I had no sympathy for Longhair Jim by
then, mind you, but I still remembered the hero he had been,
and I saw that he'd fallen a long way—not because Sallie
backed him down, but because he was so foolish as to put
himself in that position in the first place.

Finally Ben Boy said, ever so tentatively, "Don't you think he
might come looking for you, Mr. Peters?"

"I'm more afraid he'll come looking for Sallie," the cowman
said. "I've half a mind to send Ambrose up the trail without me."

"You can't," Sallie said, echoed by Dickey-bird, who exploded with a loud "No!"

Then Sallie said calmly, "He won't hurt me, but he would hurt
you, Sandy. It's better you were out of the county for a while.
Trail drive's perfect."

Sandy shook his head. "I can't leave you and these children
without protection."

Oh, for heaven's sake, I thought, who does he think has protected us all along?

"I'll get him," Dickey-bird said vehemently. "I'll just go
and . . ." His voice trailed off as he tried to decide just what he
could do to Longhair Jim. I thought his concern probably came
from a fear that he wouldn't get to go on the trail drive after all.

"Son, you'll do nothing," Sandy told him. "Sallie and I'll take
care of this. Now, all of you . . . off to bed!"

I looked at Ben Boy and then Dickey-bird, and July took my
hand, and reluctantly, we turned toward the stairs. We still
weren't used to being ordered around, but we heard authority in
Sandy's voice . . . and we liked him well enough to respect it.

July broke from my hand to run over and give Sandy a hug.
"I'm glad he didn't shoot you," she said.

"So am I, sweetheart, so am I," he said.

I lay in bed that night and swore I could hear singing coming
from the parlor, only the song wasn't about Barb'ra Allen or the
wayfaring stranger, and the voice wasn't Sallie's. Sandy Peters
was singing about when the work's all done in the fall and

another sad melody about a cowboy who went walking out on the streets of Laredo.

Next morning when we woke up Sandy Peters and Dickey-bird were gone, and Sallie was all business about getting to the store. There wasn't a word about Longhair Jim, and I never did know how she convinced Sandy Peters to go on his trail drive, but she did.

As we walked to the store that morning, Sallie sang under her breath about green growing lilacs, and I knew it was a song Sandy Peters had taught her late in the night.

Sandy Peters brought his herd down Samuels Avenue, just like he promised, and Sallie stood on the verandah like he wanted. Only, otherwise, it didn't go at all like Sandy planned.

We were all at the supper table the next night when we heard a low and distant rumble.

"Thunder?" asked Sallie.

I listened for a long minute and said, "No, cattle."

"Sandy's herd," Ben Boy declared, rushing up from the table.

By the time we got outside, we could hear cowboys yelling and cattle bawling, and we could smell the dust kicked up by the great moving body of animals as they lumbered by at a walk. Sallie put her hand over her mouth and the other hand over her eyes as though to shade them.

"It's awful!" she said.

"Think about the men who ride drag," Ben Boy said, knowing full well she didn't know about point and drag. To his everlasting disappointment, she was so busy trying to blow and brush dust away, she never even asked.

True to Sandy's word, the crew had the cattle under pretty good control, and it looked like they'd amble right down the middle of Samuels Avenue with no damage done to Sallie's fence or garden.

Then, through the dust and confusion, I saw Dickey-bird ride by, waving furiously, desperate to make sure we saw him. Intent on making us notice him, he paid no attention to where he was riding or what he was doing. Showing off, he let out an ear-splitting "Yippee-yi-ooh!" or something that sounded that way. I knew he thought that was what cowboys did.

The cattle, however, had different thoughts, and the strange, high-pitched sound from Dickey-bird was all it took to spook them. One minute they were a peaceful herd moving along, and the next they were a wave of panicked animals stampeding toward the crossing, several of them breaking loose on either side to run riot through fences, gardens, and whatever else stood in their way.

Sallie stared in dismay as the rose bushes along the fence—and then the fence itself—gave way before the uncontrollable surge of frenzied energy. "Stop them!" she cried to no one in particular.

"They're tryin'," I said, pointing to Judd Ambrose, who rode up along the side of the herd, flapping his hat and hollering, trying to channel the cattle into the road. He was successful, but it was too late for Sallie's roses.

When the herd passed, Sandy Peters rode back and stared at the fence. "Guess this wasn't such a good idea after all," he said. "I . . . well, I thought . . . Sallie had never seen a herd of cattle and I thought . . ." He seemed unable to say what he had thought. "I can't stop to fix the fence, but if you get it fixed, I'll sure pay the bill."

Sallie just smiled at him. "I'll fix the fence," she said. "It was probably worth the fence to see a cattle drive, and I thank you for coming by our house."

That was such an unexpected reaction that for a minute I thought Sandy Peters might fall off his horse. But then he waved his hat in the air and smiled and said, "See you all in the fall. Be good."

"You, too," Sallie said softly, and turned into the house singing about that cowboy that walked out on the streets of Laredo. Only this time, in her version, he was on the streets of Fort Worth.

· · · ·

Life settled down into a routine, and spring wore into summer. We got the fence repaired—Ben Boy turned out to be
pretty handy with a hammer—and Sallie and I planted new rose
bushes. She said they'd probably bloom by August when Sandy
Peters rode back, and she'd show him the damage wasn't permanent.

July and I spent all day at the store, every day except Sunday
when Sallie insisted we go to church, a new wrinkle that Ben
Boy and I accepted only reluctantly, though July loved the singing and practically begged to go every Sunday morning.

Ben Boy still went out shining shoes, but I could see that
Sallie was campaigning against that and whether Ben Boy knew
it or not, his days of freedom were doomed.

"He'd be much better off working in the store," she said to me
one day, "and I'm just going to have to insist."

So far, I hadn't seen her insist on anything and not get her
way. But I didn't tell Ben Boy that. I figured he'd have to deal
with it when the time came.

Meantime, he still brought word from the streets. One day it
was that Lulabelle had closed her house and was leaving the
Acre.

"When?" I asked.

"Three, four days. Soon as she can get everything together,"
he said. "Most the girls are gone, but 'Phronie's still there with
her."

That, I thought, was a blessing, for I doubted that Lulabelle
could have made herself toast.

"Sallie, I got to go to the Acre," I said the next morning.

Absently, she replied, "Of course not, Lizzie. I won't hear of
you going down there. You've made me promise not to go
alone, and . . ."

"That's because you don't know the Acre like I do. I *got* to go
this time. I got to say good-bye to Lulabelle."

"Mrs. Browning? She's leaving? Can't she come see you? I . . .
I don't like you to be in that part of town."

"She might could, but she won't. And I lived in that part of town for near fourteen years. One more hour isn't going to hurt me," I said in exasperation.

"Don't take July," she said, as though that were her last defense.

"I doubt Lulabelle wants to see July," I said, "but that reminds me that I ought to take July to visit Nellie Straight someday soon."

Sallie just nodded, and I left before she could issue any more warnings about the Acre. Walking down Rusk Street was a strange experience. I passed all the familiar sights, but now it seemed like a long time ago that I'd lived in the shack and begged for apples and slightly spoiled beef. Uncle Billy Winder's Cattle Exchange was familiar and yet, oh, so strange. Before I went into Lulabelle's, I walked around to the shack.

To my surprise, it was as neat and clean as I'd left it, and blankets piled in one corner told me someone was living there. The pot I'd cooked in was still outside, and there was a lone fresh apple sitting on the crate that served as a table. It almost made me homesick.

"Come slummin'?" An angry, belligerent voice jarred me out of my nostalgic mood.

"No, Chance Coker, I didn't come slummin' and I didn't come to visit you. I come to see Lulabelle."

"Didn't know Miz McNutt would let you wander this far," he said sarcastically. "I thought you pretty much had to do what she told you to."

"That's not so," I said. "I can do what I want . . . and I want to say good-bye to Lulabelle 'fore she leaves." I looked long and hard at him. "How're you doin', Chance?"

"Oh, I get by just fine," he said cockily. "Course I miss the money Lambreth used to give me. No thanks to you."

Chance was just baiting me, and I ignored him. He knew as well as I did that I had nothing—well, almost nothing—to do with Walter Lambreth's death. I changed the subject. "You livin' here alone?"

"For the time being. Some snowbird'll turn up, but I won't take in anyone weak like that Dickey-bird you all let live here."

"He's gone north on a trail drive," I said.

Chance felt the same envy Ben Boy and I had, and he was poor at disguising it. "A trail drive? How could he?"

So I told him the story of Judd Ambrose and Sandy Peters and how Dickey-bird had gone to live with them, and then Chance began to question me about life with Sallie, and I told him about the house with all its bedrooms and the food we ate and all, and he never once was sarcastic. He just kind of listened, which was something Chance Coker never did before.

"Well," I said awkwardly, "I got to go in and see Lulabelle."

"Sure," Chance said. "Come back any time . . . that is, any time you can get away from Miz McNutt."

"Chance," I said sternly, "it isn't like that."

Lulabelle was in a flurry, lumbering from one side of her bedroom to the other, picking up this gauzy garment and that, moving things from one place to the other, and not accomplishing a thing.

"Oh, Lizzie, I worried so about you. I . . . I just feel like I haven't lived up to your ma's trust in me. I told her I'd take care of you . . . and . . ."

"You took just fine care of me," I lied, "and now I got a really good place to live. I'm all right, Lulabelle, I really am."

"You sure you won't go to California with me? Girl like you, why we could make . . ."

"No, Lulabelle, I'm not ever goin' into that kind of work," I said firmly.

"No need to be huffy about it, Lizzie. I just asked."

"Yes, ma'am," I said and turned to leave. "Lulabelle, I hope you like California . . . and . . . thanks for everything you did for me and Ben Boy and July."

Layers of protection dropped from Lulabelle before my eyes. "I didn't do anything, Lizzie Jones, and you know it. And what I would have done wouldn't have been good for you. You go on and get out of here . . . and, child, you make yourself a life. You got a chance now."

I almost hugged her, but I figured that would embarrass both of us. On the way out, I stopped to steal a biscuit from 'Phronie. She must have baked a whole batch just for Lulabelle since there wasn't no one else in the house but the two of them. And I gave 'Phronie the hug that maybe I should have given Lulabelle.

And then I turned my back on the Acre and headed uptown for McNutt and Company Mercantile Store. I didn't even look back.

Chance Coker turned his back on the Acre not a week later. He showed up at Sallie's door—at suppertime, of course—and stood there, looking awkward and ill at ease, which didn't come naturally to Chance. But the blanket roll he carried, which obviously contained all his things, was a clear indication of why he'd come.

"You're the boy who tried to snatch my purse," Sallie said.

Chance cringed. "Yes, ma'am, but I'm sorry about it. I wouldn't have done it if I'd known you was a friend of Lizzie's."

"You shouldn't snatch anyone's purse" came the firm reply.

Chance hung his head and said nothing.

"Chance Coker," I said, coming from behind Sallie, "what're you doin' here? Are you lookin' for a place to light?"

"Aw, Lizzie," he said plaintively, "it ain't the same in the Acre without you all."

I delighted in seeing Chance on the spot, and so did Ben Boy, who simply stood in the doorway, never offering a word to help Chance out of his predicament. It was Sallie who spoke next.

"You best come in and have some supper," she said briskly.

Chance muttered his thanks and edged through the door, eyeing Ben Boy as though he wasn't sure he wouldn't throw him out.

"We have rules," Sallie announced firmly. "They begin with washing up for dinner—at the basin out the back door—and they go right on through studying and staying in the house at night."

"Yes, ma'am," Chance muttered.

"You got to follow those rules, Chance Coker," I said. Sallie might trust him, but I knew Chance too well.

"Lizzie . . ." Sallie protested. "I'm sure the young man understands."

I gave her a black look and went back to dishing up the chicken pie we were having for supper.

Chance moved in with Ben Boy, though neither of them was happy about it, and pretty soon he was part of our family. I have to give him credit—Chance adapted. He went out shining shoes with Ben Boy, and they learned to share the territory rather than scrapping over it, and each one brought back his earnings. I never did hear about Chance picking another pocket or grabbing another purse, but for at least a year I was ever watchful. And he never tried to sneak out at night, but I guess he never had emergencies like Ben Boy and me.

By the end of the summer, Sallie had added Idabelle to our ranks. A pale, brown-haired girl of ten, she was sitting on a street corner when Sallie found her. Her hair looked like it needed a good washing, and her dress was worn, mended and patched to make it smaller. Obviously, it was somebody's hand-me-down and whoever made it over didn't sew like Sallie did.

When asked, Idabelle admitted to having a pa who farmed a piece of land east of town. He was shopping, she said, but when Sallie asked her close, it was obvious that he was somewhere in the Acre and the only thing he was buying was beer.

"And where's your ma?" Sallie had asked.

"Dead." That single-word reply loosed a torrent of tears in the poor child, and pretty soon it appeared that the father beat the girl and blamed her for the mother's death. "Pa says he'd be better off if'n I died too," the poor thing wailed, absolutely capturing Sallie's heart. Grabbing Idabelle by the hand, Sallie went in search of the father, who, when confronted, said he'd be "confounded glad" for someone to take "that brat girl" off his hands. Sallie obliged.

I could have been angry about it on several counts, among them that Sallie'd promised not to go traipsing around the Acre alone, even during the day, especially after she forbad me to go there. If she expected me to mind her about things she knew better than me, then I expected her to listen when I knew more than she did—and I definitely knew more about the Acre.

"Remember that hide hunter?" I asked, and she bowed her head and admitted she should have come for me first.

"Next time," she promised, but I hoped to heaven she wouldn't find another child and have to go searching for another drunken father in the Acre.

Then, of course, Idabelle had to share a room with July and me. That didn't please me a whole lot, but I tried for Sallie's sake to be nice. July was downright niggardly about making room, but I walloped her one when Sallie wasn't looking and after that, she behaved better toward Idabelle. Some old habits die hard, 'specially when they work.

Idabelle didn't take up much room and she was quiet, hardly saying a word. Sometimes I forgot she was there, so I didn't mind her being around too much, but when it proved that she was twice as good at sums as me—though four years younger— my anger came on strong.

And then there was Tom, Just Plain Tom, who came to the store one morning looking for swamping work. "Hey, Chance, Ben Boy," he said, greeting them by name, and then looking shyly at me. "Lizzie?"

"Hey, Tom," I said. We all knew Tom. He and his ma lived in one of the cribs behind Lulabelle's, and Tom spent a good deal of his time locked out on the streets, because his ma was busy. Tom was younger than us and never had made much at working the streets. We used to see him just sitting on the curb, waiting for his ma to tell him he could come home, and Ben Boy and I were both a bit scornful 'cause we thought he should have been shining shoes or doing something rather than just sitting there. Neither pity nor compassion was in our vocabulary.

Pale and blond with dark circles under listless blue eyes, Tom didn't look any stronger to me than Dickey-bird had, and I doubted he'd sweep up to my satisfaction. Besides, I could see the future written clear on the wall—he'd end up living in the McNutt house, and I thought there were enough of us already. Maybe one too many, I thought, looking at Chance.

"You ever swamped?" I asked Tom, before Sallie came sailing forth from her office when she heard there was a boy looking for work.

"Sallie," I whispered in her ear, "we can't be takin' in every-one who asks."

"And why not?" she asked loud as you please. Then, more softly, she said, "Lizzie, you mind the store. I've got to go see about that poor boy's mother."

"You aren't goin' to the Acre alone," I said, reaching for the bonnet she insisted I wear now that it was full summer and the sun hot enough to fry an egg on the streets. Sallie claimed I had to protect my complexion, a nicety no one had ever mentioned to me before. "You promised."

"I want you to mind the store," she said directly. "Chance will go with me to the Acre. Will that fulfill our bargain?"

I reckoned as how it would, and I guessed, even to myself, that I didn't mind too much if I got to tend the store.

When she came back, Sallie was carrying a bundle of clothes. I knew without asking what was about to happen. "Tom," she said, "come into my office." I sorely wanted to eavesdrop but Sallie'd taught me some things about honesty, and I couldn't have faced her if she'd caught me. So I waited until they came out, Sallie's arm around Tom and his face tear-streaked.

"Just Plain Tom's mother is going away for a while," Sallie said, "and he's going to stay with us. I know you'll make him welcome."

Later she told me that Tom's mother was going back to her parents' farm in East Texas, but the grandparents didn't even

know about Tom, there being no father and all that, and there
was no one there to care for him.

"She goin' home to die?" I asked bluntly.

"Probably," Sallie said, shaking her head, "but we don't have
to say that to Tom."

Much to our surprise, Just Plain Tom's mother, in good health,
came for him after about a month, said they were both going
home to live on the farm. They'd had enough of city life, she
laughed, and I plain ached with jealousy when I saw them walk
away together. What I wanted was someone who wanted to
take care of me, like she obviously was going to take care of
Tom. Oh, Ma, where were you?

Ben Boy never did get used to sharing his room, though.
When he came home the first night Tom was with us, he demanded, "What're we running here? A blasted orphanage?"

"Maybe so," Sallie said, "maybe so." And then she began to
sing about the green growing lilacs while she mended a pair of
Ben Boy's pants that had given out at the knee.

I knew then that neither Idabelle nor Tom would be the last in
a long line of us to come and go. But I also knew that Ben Boy,
July, and I were special—and we wouldn't be going anywhere. I
guess what I didn't recognize was that from Sallie I had the same
caring that Tom had from his mother—maybe surer. I didn't
need to be jealous of any Acre brat, but I didn't know that yet.

The whole summer went by without a word from Longhair
Jim, and I was foolish enough to think we were rid of him
forever. Course I'd thought that once before—when Stephen
McNutt's murder was solved—and I'd been wrong. But from
April to August is a long time, and by mid-August I figured he'd
forgotten Sallie. Ben Boy and Chance told us that Longhair Jim
was still sitting in this saloon and that, getting sloppy drunk and
ruining whatever was left of his reputation as a hero. If I'd had
him before me, I think I'd have shaken him. Heroes shouldn't
act like that.

But as August drew to a close I was more worried about

Sandy Peters. I'd catch Sallie staring off toward the Cold Spring crossing as though she expected to see someone ride out of the prairie—and I knew full well it was Sandy she expected.

If I understood how these things went, Sandy'd marry her and take her to his ranch to live. I'd seen well enough how they looked at each other, and I just figured they couldn't bear to be apart anymore. And if Sallie went to live on a ranch, she'd sell the McNutt house, and we'd all be back in the shack in the Acre. Only now there was two more of us. I had nightmares about trying to steal enough food for five and keeping Chance honest and Ben Boy happy and July safe and teaching Idabelle more about survival than she seemed to know.

No, I wasn't looking forward to seeing Sandy Peters ride in. But then again, I sure hoped Longhair Jim had forgotten his quarrel with him.

Meantime, Sallie sat on the verandah in the evenings and sang about the work being all done in the fall.

Twelve

LONGHAIR JIM strolled into the store one day in August. I heard Sallie groan softly, and I thought maybe she'd remind him that she'd told him never to set foot in the store again. But I guess that was a little strong, even for Sallie.

She was polite but distant when he came back to her desk and draped his long body over the top so that he was kind of leaning toward her. Well, she did pull back in her chair some, but she managed to smile and greet him.

"And a good day to you, too," he said expansively. "It's a fine day, it really is."

I wondered if he was breathing whisky all over her.

"Yessir, things are really looking up," he said, leaving the desk to stroll casually around. He looped his hands through his belt, pulling back his jacket to reveal the double holsters he always wore. "Got myself a new partner."

"Oh?" Sallie asked, while I wanted to shout, "Mr. McIntyre again?"

"Yep, man named Charley Bull. We're reviving the detecting business." He spoke confidently, and yet, I thought I saw a slight hint of fear in his eyes.

"Well," Sallie said brightly, "I certainly hope things go well for you."

"You'll be the first to know," he said, leering over the desktop at her. "I got great plans . . . and you—"

Sallie cut off his sentence abruptly. "Mr. Courtright, I certainly have heard a lot about your wife. I understand she has great talent as a shootist."

He looked startled. "Yeah, she's pretty good." Then he puffed up. " 'Course I taught her all she knows. She wasn't but fourteen when we married."

Sallie gulped a little, and then sailed bravely ahead. "And she supported your children while you were, ah, away?"

"Well, now, I wouldn't exactly say that. . . ." The conversation was not going the way Longhair Jim had wanted it to, and he changed the subject abruptly. "Peters back from up north yet?"

"I wouldn't know," Sallie lied, for if he had been back, she'd have been the first to know.

"I haven't forgot he tried to disgrace me," Courtright said petulantly. "He had no call to treat me the way he did. I'll be around." And with that he turned on his heel and left.

"Sallie!" I exclaimed as soon as he was out of earshot. "Sandy Peters never did anything to him. You were the one that disgraced him."

"Jim Courtright," she said thoughtfully, "has a selective memory. He remembers things conveniently rather than accurately."

"And he's still after Sandy?"

"I don't know," she said unhappily.

"He's dangerous!" I exploded, as though the realization had just come to me. Longhair Jim had gone from hero to failure and, now, to outright menace in my mind. How were Ben Boy and I going to protect Sallie and Sandy . . . and all of us . . . from him?

Turned out we didn't have to do the protecting, though we didn't know it at the time.

Sandy and Dickey-bird came back from their trail drive, Dickey-bird so full of his adventures that I was cross and wouldn't listen to him. Ben Boy hung on every word, until I kicked his shin and told him I had important things to talk to him about. And then Dickey-bird looked so hurt that I felt guilty.

But after one day, they rode on out to Sandy's spread, and I heaved a great sigh of relief.

"Sallie," I asked tentatively, a day or so later, as she and I walked along Belknap. July was visiting Mrs. Straight, and Idabelle, Chance, and Ben Boy had been left to clean the house on Samuels—much to the boys' disgust.

"Don't you . . . well, you know, don't you miss Sandy?"

"Of course I do," she said, as though she couldn't imagine why I was asking. "I like him very much."

Yeah, I thought glumly, and you'll move out to his ranch if he asks you.

"Would you . . . I mean . . . well, have you ever thought about living on a ranch?" This conversation was not going well.

Suddenly, she stopped in the midst of the sidewalk, turned to face me, and laughed that deep, wonderful laugh of hers. "Lizzie Jones," she said, "are you asking me if I'd ever marry Sandy Peters?"

"Yes, ma'am, I guess I am," I said miserably.

"Well, the answer is yes, if he asks me," she said, "but don't you tell him."

"I won't," I muttered, as unhappy as I could be.

She stared at me as we started walking again. "That doesn't please you?"

"Oh . . . if that's what you want. . . ." What could I say?

She thought for a moment, and then seemed to see it clear. "You're afraid I'll leave you, aren't you?"

"Yes," I admitted under my breath.

"Lizzie, you still don't understand me, do you?" She stopped, pulled me to one side, and faced me straight. "Look me in the eye," she commanded.

Reluctantly, I did as I was told.

"I will not leave you or Ben Boy or July, or any of you. I've made myself a promise . . . and whether you know it or not, I've made a promise to you. You're going to grow up in a regular household . . . and next month, you're going to start back to school."

She kind of snuck that one in on me, but I was too occupied with the rest of the conversation to react much.

"I don't know why you can't understand and accept that," she said, shaking her head.

How could I tell her that no one ever had given me reason to trust, not till she came along, and it was still a new experience. I'd learned not to count on anyone but myself. Why, even my greatest hero had turned into a drunken troublemaker who threatened to shoot innocent people. But it was beginning to dawn on me that I could trust Sallie in a way that I'd never trusted before. She'd been in Fort Worth near eight months, but it seemed like a lifetime. And I knew, when I got right down to considering it, that she'd taught me new things in that lifetime.

She started walking, humming "Green Grow the Lilacs" under her breath and almost ignoring me as I hurried to catch up with her. But as she turned to unlock the store, she said, "You know, Lizzie, we can't ever be sure about much. I never thought I'd be running a store in Texas and raising five children, but here I am . . . and we can't tell where any of us will be two or three years from now. But I promise you—we'll be together."

"Yes, ma'am," I said, and I was content with it. I believed her.

Idabelle loved school. She was dressed and ready to go each morning before the rest of us could get our shoes buttoned, and she brought home paper after paper with "100" written on it. Sallie beamed and posted the papers in a special place on the kitchen wall. I began to hate Idabelle for more than her taking half of my bed and part of July's affection, but I managed to do all right in school. It was just that I was older than most of my schoolmates, and sometimes I heard them snicker behind my back when I couldn't cipher a sentence.

One girl went so far as to mutter something about "Acre brats," but Ben Boy told her if she ever said anything like that he'd cut off her curls with his penknife—I thought it was an unusual and fairly clever threat—and she quieted right down. When he grabbed her arm and made her apologize, she kind of

muttered, but she never said anything after that . . . and neither did any of the others.

Chance and Ben Boy resented school mightily, both wanting
to be back out on the streets. Chance, in fact, took to skipping
school to return to the Acre—"got to find out what's happenin',"
he said—but Sallie soon found out and told him he could either
live in her house and go to school or go back to the Acre perma-
nently and do what he wanted. He started right back to school,
though I know giving in cost his pride, and we never teased him
about it.

Besides, the Acre just wasn't the same. Even Ben Boy said so
after he took his shoeshine box in that direction a Saturday or
two. "Lulabelle's house is empty," he reported, "and Uncle
Billy's place looks like it's gonna fall down. Uncle Billy says he's
got no customers."

"Lulabelle always said reform would get the Acre," I said
knowingly.

"Uncle Billy says its farmers, not reform," Ben Boy laughed.
"Says now that the cowboys and hide hunters go west of here,
all we get is farmers . . . and they don't drink and gamble at
all. Dull, that's what they are."

"Do you miss it, Ben Boy?" I asked.

"Yeah," he said, "I do. I even miss the shack and those awful
meals you used to cook."

I took out after him, and he ran so fast that I never had a
chance to tell him I missed those times too. The Acre was a
bittersweet memory for me.

All that winter, Chance or Ben Boy brought back reports on
Longhair Jim, as though we were interested or something.

"Running a protection racket, so I hear," Chance said scornfully. "Thinks he can shake down the likes of Luke Short and
them."

"I thought he and his partner were operating a detective
agency," Sallie said, looking up from the table where she was
supervising July's penmanship.

"They are," Chance explained. "Longhair Jim goes to the owner of a gambling hall and tells him that, for a fee, the T. I. Courtright Commercial Detective Agency will see that there's no trouble in their place."

"And people pay him?" she asked incredulously.

"Sure," Chance said. "Folks in the Acre do most anything to keep the law away from them . . . and they remember Longhair Jim's good with those pistols. They're used to paying . . . and they get their money back from the suckers. But he ain't gonna have no luck with Luke Short," he predicted darkly. "I hear Luke Short told him to jump in the Trinity."

"Isn't going to have any luck," Sallie said automatically, while I remembered those green eyes and the cold look that Short had given Courtright the day Sallie took me to the White Elephant.

Longhair Jim hadn't been in the store since the day Sallie'd asked him about his wife, and the one time I'd seen him on the street, I'd ducked and gone the other way. Ben Boy and Chance reported that he was drinking heavily, in this saloon and that, and bragging even more heavily about the prosperity of his detective agency. But he was, I thought, out of our lives . . . and I breathed a sigh of relief for that.

Sallie made a festival out of Christmas, such a grand and happy occasion that I thought life could never be any better. Judd and Sandy and Dickey-bird came in the day before Christmas, to stay at Peer's House so they could spend all Christmas Day with us. And the night before, there were ten stockings hung on our mantel. Next morning, each stocking had an orange, a freshly baked sugar cookie, and a piece of peppermint candy.

There were presents under the tree for everyone: a hand-knit scarf for Sandy Peters, a warm woolen shirt for each of the boys, and a new belt for Judd Ambrose—Sallie'd seen him eyeing them in the store. Each of us girls received a new flannel nightgown—when had Sallie done all that sewing without our knowing?—and a pair of gloves.

None of us were much at giving Christmas gifts—it had always been just another day in the Acre—but we had sensed that it was an important holiday for Sallie. Of course, we can't claim to have been too smart to discover that. For two weeks beforehand, Sallie baked pies and cakes, made cookies and candy.

"Lizzie, isn't there someplace in the Acre that you can take these cookies so the other children there can share them?"

"You want me to go to the Acre?" I asked incredulously.

"If you take Chance or Ben Boy with you," she said, serenely ignoring the sarcasm in my voice.

I didn't like her idea, 'cause it seemed to me that cookies would only bring us more residents. Once someone on the street in the Acre tasted those cookies and figured out there was more food where they came from, Sallie's front door would be battered down with people wanting to live with us.

In the long run, we compromised, and Ben Boy and I took the cookies to the Baptist church, where they would be distributed.

But back to Christmas morning. Ben Boy and Chance had shined shoes early and late on weekends, and I'd saved my quarters from working at the store, but we didn't have near enough for what we wanted.

"Dickey-bird," I said one day in November when he and Sandy were in town, "you got to help."

"Sure," he said. "I got four quarters."

"You go on a trail drive, and all you've got is four quarters?" I asked in disgust.

"I didn't spend much," he whined, "but I bought myself this scarf. . . ." He pointed proudly to the bandana around his neck.

"And the hat?" I asked.

"Judd bought that," he said defensively.

In the end, Sandy Peters chipped in a whole lot of money to make up for what we lacked. He swore us to secrecy, until I told him we wouldn't go through with our plan if he didn't own up to his part in it, and he finally gave in. Then he and Judd had to do the lifting and hauling to complete our surprise.

Christmas morning, when Sallie came into the parlor, there stood a melodeon. Granted, it was not new and the finish was a little scratched and chipped, but the tone was perfect and it had a scrollwork music stand on it and a brocade-covered stool in front of it.

"Oh!" Sallie said, and then, again, "Oh!"

I never had seen her speechless before, and when I looked again, I realized I'd never seen tears in her eyes before. But there she was, crying and laughing all at once.

"What can I say?" she asked. "You shouldn't have . . . it . . . it's too much."

"Play a Christmas song," Sandy told her, and she played more than one, singing "Oh Come All Ye Faithful" and "Silent Night" and something about a boar's head—"a pig's head?" I asked Ben Boy, but he just shrugged.

"Sing with me," she urged, and Sandy raised a tentative tenor but the rest of us stood silent, except for July, who joined in with a clear, sweet soprano in "Silent Night." She'd been following Sallie around the store, memorizing the song and singing it to herself. One thing about July, she learned things quickly and had a good memory.

"You don't know the songs, do you?" Sallie asked us, unbelievingly.

We shook our heads, and she went back to her singing with a vengeance. Like July, we'd be learning them, I knew.

Nellie Straight came for Christmas dinner, protesting all the while that she should be cooking. But we made her sit in the parlor like company until dinner was on the table at noon. Sallie had cooked a huge meal—though I have to claim some credit for helping her—and the table was laden with a wild turkey and a boiled ham, corn pudding, pickles that Nellie had put up, sweet potato pie and apple pie from dried apples, and for dessert, two cakes, one of them a six-layer jam cake. We ate until we thought we'd burst.

"I wonder," said Sallie as we still sat at the table, "if the Court-rights are having a fine Christmas. I hope so."

I thought it was odd for her to think of Longhair Jim at a time like that, but then I reasoned that he had, welcome or not, been a big part of our lives the past year. And I remembered that I owed him my life—well, sort of.

And then I got to thinking of all the changes in our lives in the past year, and it almost made me teary-eyed. When I caught Ben Boy staring at me, I told him gruffly to start clearing the table. But Sallie caught me, too, and she came over and put an arm around me.

"It's all right to feel sentimental, Lizzie, it really is." She had a tear in her eye, too.

Winter was mean that year. A great blizzard swept the plains, leaving cattlemen—including Sandy Peters—with devastating losses. Cattle drifted south, trying to get out of the storm, and some were never returned to their home range in spite of a big roundup that all the cattlemen cooperated in. Other cattle were found across the range, frozen in drifts.

In Fort Worth, the wind howled and blew just like it did on the prairies, and many a night as I sat snug in Sallie's house I shuddered to think what this winter would have been like in the shack. But we were safe and secure, warm and well fed.

"Ben Boy," I said, "aren't we lucky?"

He gave me a queer look, like he thought I was getting soft in the head, crying at Christmas dinner and staring out at snow-storms.

By early February, though, the snow had blown itself out, and the rains set in, turning most streets into thick rivers of mud and making all our tempers a little short.

"Ben Boy, do you have to fidget every minute?" I asked, as we sat around the dining table doing our studies. He'd shift in his chair, put his head on his elbow, then raise up and twist around, until it made me itch to watch him.

"I can't help it," he muttered. "If you knew . . ."

"Knew what?" I asked in disgust, while Idabelle said righteously, "Can you two *please* be quiet?"

Chance looked at Ben Boy and then at me with a slight grin that said he knew a secret.

"All right, you two," I exploded. "What's goin' on?"

"Shhh!" they whispered in unison, pointing toward the kitchen, where Sallie was cooking supper, with July singing to her about the poor cowboy who was all wrapped in white linen.

First Ben Boy, then Chance, casually got up from the table and wandered into the parlor. Soon as I was sure Idabelle's nose was buried in her books again, I followed.

"All right," I demanded in a loud whisper, "what is it?"

"Longhair Jim," Ben Boy said. "He's been drinkin' all week and talkin' in the saloons, saying there was a conspiracy"—he puzzled the strange word out carefully—"against him at the White Elephant. Said he hadn't been shown any respect, and he was gonna settle it once and for all."

"Settle it?" I echoed.

"Yeah," Chance said, "with a peacemaker. When I was shining shoes, I overheard him in John Stewart's saloon telling Old Man McCarty that some men might be stronger than others but the Colt made all men equal."

I drew in my breath sharply. The enmity between Longhair Jim and Luke was fast reaching the point where neither man could back down.

Ben Boy was anxious to add to the story. "What's really scary," he blurted, "is that Longhair Jim told McCarty that he'd lived over his time. Lizzie, I think he means to call out Luke Short."

"Sounds like it," I said. We knew about calling a man out, but aside from Longhair Jim's botched attempt to shoot it out with Sandy Peters, I'd never seen the real thing. The old Acre-bred obsession to be in on the action was beginning to grab hold of me, and I could see that Ben Boy and Chance were already fast in its clutch.

"We're gonna sneak out tonight," Ben Boy said, "Chance and me."

"I'm goin' too," I protested.

"You can't," Chance said. "You're a girl."

"That never bothered you before," I retorted.

"No, but it'd bother Sallie," Ben Boy said smugly. I guess it made him feel superior to think I'd have to stay home.

For just a minute there, I'd forgotten about Sallie and where we were. I was back in the Acre, free to do as I pleased, and ready for any and all excitement. But Ben Boy stopped me, and I remembered, unhappily, the railroad strike and my awful dilemma. It was the same this time, though I didn't need Sallie to tell me I couldn't go. I knew it myself.

"Lizzie," Ben Boy pleaded, "don't tell Sallie. Tell her . . ." His voice trailed off as he tried to think of a good story.

"I forgot my shoeshine box," Chance said, "and I didn't want to go back alone to get it."

"Scared?" I asked sarcastically, and he raised his hand as though to smack me.

"I ain't scared, but you can tell her that." Even that cost him some pride.

"I'm not lyin'," I said. "Best I'll do is say you had an errand, and you'll be back soon."

They mumbled their thanks, grabbed sweaters and caps, and were out the door.

When Sallie called for supper, they weren't back. She was close to the angriest she ever got. "Suppertime! They know enough to be here for supper," she fumed.

"Yes, ma'am," I said. "Must've been an important errand."

Idabelle gave me a stern look but said nothing. July, though, sang out, "I bet Lizzie knows where they are, don't you, Lizzie?" I could have strangled her, but I settled for a threatening look that said she'd get it when we got to our bedroom if she wasn't quiet. She didn't say any more. July was getting to be a regular little goody-two-shoes.

It was a long evening. We ate chicken and dumplings in silence, and did the dishes with no more talk than "That plate isn't quite clean, July" or "Idabelle, hang that towel out to dry now." Then we girls settled down to our mending. Sallie insisted we had to be good seamstresses, another thing that frequently made me think the differences between boys and girls were not at all fair.

Sallie sewed a stitch or two, then got up to peer out the window, then went back to her sewing. Finally, she gave it up and began to pace. Outside, a cold rain fell steadily.

"Out in this rain!" she said. "They'll catch their death."

I found a certain satisfaction in the fact that they'd at least be wet and miserable, but I kept sewing, my eyes down, though inside I was burning with curiosity.

"If only I had someone to send to look for them. . . ."

"I'll go," I volunteered, a little too quickly.

"No, Lizzie, that's not appropriate. Oh me, at times like these I wish for Sandy or Judd . . . and if they're not around, I almost wish I hadn't chased Longhair Jim away."

Too late to wish that, I thought grimly.

It was the longest evening I'd ever spent. Stephen McNutt's grandfather clock ticked each second slowly and deliberately, and the hour came when July was sent to bed, then Idabelle, and finally only Sallie and I remained at the dining table, me working on my sewing and her drumming her fingers on the table. The rain stopped around eight, started again around nine.

"Lizzie? Are they all right?"

"Yes, ma'am," I said. "I'm sure they are."

Just then we heard shouts and footsteps, and both boys, dripping wet, burst into the kitchen. They stood there, creating a huge puddle, and babbled at once.

"Quiet!" Sallie demanded. "We can't understand you. Now what is it, Chance?"

"Longhair Jim's dead," he panted. "Luke Short shot him."

The news, expected though it was, washed over me like a tidal wave, and for just a moment I had to hold on to the cabinet. Sallie turned white as anything, her eyes round and horrified.

"Dead?" she echoed.

"Yes, ma'am," they chorused. And then the story came out. Longhair Jim went to the White Elephant and spoke to Jake Johnson, Luke's partner. They stood outside—it wasn't raining right then—and pretty soon, Jake went inside to get Short. Ben Boy and Chance knew all this because they were hiding across the street, well out of sight in a doorway. They could see and hear, but they couldn't be seen—and they darn sure kept quiet so no one would hear *them*.

Short came out, and the three men stood there talking.

"Longhair Jim accused Luke Short of trying to put him in a bad light," Chance said, "and Short told him that he hadn't always been friendly. But they didn't seem mad or nothin'. Jake Johnson, though, he sure seemed nervous, lookin' from one to the other of those two and then looking like he wished he was someplace far away."

"And then," Ben Boy interrupted, "Luke Short, he reached to straighten his vest—you know how men do," and he demonstrated, pretending to smooth a nonexistent vest. "Longhair Jim, he was so drunk he thought Short was drawin' on him. He said, 'Don't you pull a gun on me!' "

"What'd Luke Short do?" I asked, impatient with their telling.

"Told him he didn't have a gun and raised his vest to prove it," Chance said, "but Longhair Jim, seems like he was determined to die. He pulled his gun anyway."

"On an unarmed man?" Sallie asked, and we all three stared at her in amazement. How could she be so dumb?

"He wasn't unarmed," Chance said scornfully. "He always had a pistol in a special pocket in his pants, leather-lined for fast draw."

"But if Longhair Jim drew first . . ." She was having trouble understanding.

Ben Boy shrugged. "Luke Short was faster . . . his first shot hit Longhair Jim's thumb, and 'fore Jim could border shift to the other hand, Luke fired again. Had his gun right up against Longhair Jim by then."

Sallie shrieked in horror, but Ben Boy said, "Sallie, it was shoot Longhair Jim or be shot himself."

She nodded numbly. "Then what?"

Chance managed a smile. "All hell broke loose." Sallie didn't even reprimand him for his language. "Longhair Jim fell right into the doorway of Ella Blackwell's shooting gallery. Lucky thing Mrs. Courtright wasn't working right then. People appeared from all over, and finally Bony Tucker—he's a policeman—came up. Longhair Jim was dying, and I saw Tucker whisperin' to him, but I don't know what they said."

"Tucker asked who'd seen what happened," Ben Boy went on, "and Jake Johnson stepped forward. Tucker asked for other witnesses, but nobody said nothin'."

"Anything," Sallie said, then, "You were witnesses. Why didn't you speak up?"

"And get mixed up in that mess? No sir," Chance said. "We'd end up in the hoosegow, just like Dickey-bird did."

She nodded absently, as though it were all too much for her to understand, but forever after I thought it was important that Ben Boy and Chance were witnesses to a shooting that everybody thought only Jake Johnson had seen.

The rest of the story wasn't as exciting. Luke Short had been taken off to jail, though Ben Boy swears he heard someone say it was for his own protection. Ben Boy and Chance followed when Longhair Jim's body was taken to his house, and as they stood outside they could hear loud sobs and wailing from Mrs. Courtright and her children.

"The poor, poor woman," Sallie said, "to have loved such a man. He led her such a life, and now this. I must go to her immediately in the morning."

To us, Mrs. Courtright was a minor player in the drama—we didn't know her, had no feel for her. But I guess it was Sallie's womanly instinct (would I ever develop that, I wondered?) that made her reach out. Next morning, she packed up bread and pies and set off for Mrs. Courtright's house, telling us to open the store as usual.

By mid-morning, she was back at the store, indignant. "That Luke Short person," she sputtered, "he went and offered to marry Mrs. Courtright and raise her children! Said he felt responsible."

"Who told you that?" I asked skeptically. It had been a slow morning, and I was sure glad something interesting was happening somewhere. I guessed nobody was shopping because everybody was off to the courthouse, where they held a special hearing about Luke Short.

"Betty told me," Sallie said. "That is, Mrs. Courtright. She's heartbroken, just heartbroken. Of course, she sent Mr. Short packing, but to think of the nerve!"

"Sallie," I said, "Luke Short's already got a wife. He's too smart to do that. Maybe she made that up."

"Lizzie!" Sallie was horrified.

Luke Short, arrested by a policeman—he who had been a marshal himself in the wildest towns in the Wild West—was freed on bail, in time for the funeral if he'd have wanted to go, though I don't suppose he did.

Sallie insisted that we all go to the funeral. We watched the procession make its way down Main Street and across the river to Oakwood Cemetery.

"He was our friend," she said, "no matter what kind of a man he was."

"And no matter if he was a bother?" I asked.

"Lizzie, you of all people should show some respect for Mr. Courtright," she scolded.

"Yes, ma'am," I said, and I agreed with her. Still it was hard. If he'd never been my hero, he wouldn't have fallen so far in my eyes. Chance, for instance, would never disappoint me because I never expected as much of him.

Still, when I stood in the crowd that lined Main Street I was glad Chance was no longer picking pockets, for he'd have had a field day. People stood three and four deep on the curb downtown as Fort Worth's longest funeral procession ever wound its way past us. The M. T. Johnson Hook and Ladder Company—the same ones that had rescued Jim when his horse fell while he was escaping that time—led the cortege, with a wagon and horses draped in black. Behind them were six blocks of carriages holding everyone from the mayor to Uncle Billy Winder; I suppose for the former, it was politic to go to the funeral of a local hero, and for the latter, it was a chance to be publicly respectable.

That long funeral procession bothered me some. I could have understood it if Longhair Jim had been shot down in the performance of his duties as marshal before he fled to New Mexico. But ever since he'd come back, his reputation had been questionable. He wasn't a hero in the city anymore—until he was killed. Then, suddenly, he was a hero all over again, and folks remembered that he was not only marshal but army scout, shootist, and, somehow, a person who stood for the West in their minds.

Mrs. Courtright and her children rode in a covered carriage, but we could make out the shape of them as they went by, and Sallie, holding her hand over her mouth in anguish, whispered, "Poor, poor woman."

I wanted to tell her that Longhair Jim had taken his chances and lost, something every gambler did, something we in the Acre were familiar with. He wouldn't have expected folks to feel sorry for him; tears for him were misdirected. But I sensed Sallie wouldn't understand that.

"We goin' to the cemetery?" I asked, while Chance and Ben Boy chorused, "Of course we are!"

"No," Sallie said, "it's too far to walk. We'll go back to the store." Longhair Jim was to be buried in Oakwood Cemetery—down Main Street and across the Trinity River.

"Sallie," I said, "I want to go to the cemetery."

She turned to me in surprise. "Why ever, Lizzie?"

"You said it. He was our friend." It wasn't a lie. Longhair Jim was friend, enemy, hero, and drunk, all rolled into one package. I needed to see him lowered into the ground.

To my everlasting surprise, Sallie didn't fuss about what was proper or the long walk—it wasn't any longer than many I'd made, 'cept it crossed the river, which made it seem like a journey instead of a walk. She just said, "I'll take Idabelle and July back to the store. Ben Boy, Chance, you stay close to Lizzie."

"Yes, ma'am," they sang.

And so, for one last time, we set off like the old days, the three of us following the excitement. Folks looked at us, but we were used to that. I heard a snicker or two about "Acre brats" but once I heard someone say, "No, those are Sallie McNutt's youngsters." And I held my head proud.

The cemetery was crowded, but we knew how to work a crowd, wriggling through until we were in the front, near touching distance of the black-veiled Mrs. Courtright and her three sobbing children.

And that's how I was right there when they lowered Longhair Jim Courtright's casket into a hole in the ground, and the minister said those old words, "Dust thou art, to dust thou shall return." It gave me a lump in the throat so bad I was afraid I'd cry . . . and then, for once, I didn't care if I did.

Some folks say the Acre died with Longhair Jim. A way of life was being buried, and the Wild West was gone. I didn't know about that, but as I stood there, February wind whipping my hair into my face, I cried real tears for all the things I'd lost—the Acre and Lulabelle and the freedom to run wild and be hungry and cold and take care of July and Ben Boy and, yes, even Longhair Jim Courtright, who despised me as an Acre brat but who once walked tall in my eyes. It's hard to let your heroes—and your past—go.

Ben Boy, Chance, and I walked along the north side of the river to the Cold Springs crossing, and Chance produced fifteen cents, enough to let all three of us ride the raft. Had he been picking pockets in the funeral crowd after all? I found out I didn't like not having firm ground under my feet, and I was glad when we were back on Samuels Avenue, where a warm welcome and a hot supper waited for us.

Epilogue

HELL'S HALF ACRE faded away after the death of Longhair Jim Courtright, though its disappearance can neither be directly traced to Courtright's death nor to the subsequent brutal murder of a dance-hall girl found nailed to an outhouse door one morning. No, most folks say time took care of the Acre, as the cowboys, frontiersmen, and highwaymen moved west of the city and were replaced by homeowners and businessmen. The demand for the Acre's way of life lessened, and the strength of law enforcement officials increased. The Acre operated well into the twentieth century, but it was never again the same as when Lulabelle reigned over her house, and Ben Boy and July and I lived in the Acre, and Longhair Jim Courtright was a hero. Sometimes it's hard to see your heroes die.

AUTHOR'S NOTE

Lizzie and all her friends of the Acre—Ben Boy, July, Dickey-bird, Lulabelle, 'Phronie, and Uncle Billy—are creations of my imagination, as is Sallie, though she may bear some slight resemblance to Belle Burchill, who established the first orphanage in Fort Worth. Mrs. Burchill persuaded county authorities to buy a large house at the foot of Samuels Avenue—just about where the McNutt house stands in my story—to house homeless children from the Acre. The house had formerly belonged to a well-known madam.

Stephen McNutt, Sandy Peters, Walter Lambreth, and Judd Ambrose are also fictional, but B. B. Paddock, Luke Short, and Longhair Jim Courtright are very real. Paddock was a civic-minded, crusading newspaperman who envisioned a railhead center in Fort Worth, fought for such reforms as a regular instead of a volunteer fire department, and generally loomed large in the history of the city. Luke Short was a gentleman gambler whose wanderings took him through a wide swath of the American West; ultimately, he found his best success at the White Elephant Saloon in Fort Worth, but he died at thirty-nine of kidney failure, perhaps brought on by rich living. History books tell us that Timothy Isaiah (Longhair Jim) Courtright did most of the things attributed to him in this story, except there is no record of his having shot a lawyer in the street, as he does Walter Lambreth. And there is certainly no record of Courtright ever having been talked out of a gunfight by an indignant woman.

Readers interested in Longhair Jim or in Fort Worth's wild 'n' woolly past may want to investigate the classic but lively city history, *Fort Worth: Outpost on the Trinity* by Oliver Knight (University of Oklahoma, 1952; reprinted by Texas Christian University Press, 1990, with an essay on the twentieth century by Cissy Stewart Lale), the more recent *Hell's Half Acre: Life and Legend of a Red-Light District* by Richard F. Selcer (TCU Press, 1991), or the now out-of-print biography *Luke Short and His Era* by William R. Cox.

ABOUT THE AUTHOR

Judy Alter admits to a particular interest in local history; Fort Worth, Texas—the setting of *A Ballad for Sallie*—has been her home for twenty-five years. The author of eight novels, she is currently director of Texas Christian University Press and is a former president of the Western Writers of America. Her previous Double D Western, *Mattie,* was awarded the Western Writers of America Spur Award as the best Western novel of the year.